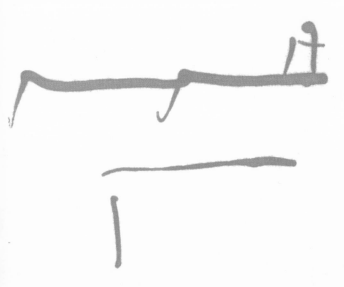

T0155051

THE
BAUDELAIRE
FRACTAL

LISA
ROBERTSON

COACH HOUSE BOOKS, TORONTO

first edition

Canada Council   Conseil des Arts
for the Arts   du Canada

ONTARIO ARTS COUNCIL
CONSEIL DES ARTS DE L'ONTARIO
an Ontario government agency
un organisme du gouvernement de l'Ontario

Canada

Published with the generous assistance of the Canada Council for the Arts and the Ontario Arts Council. Coach House Books also acknowledges the support of the Government of Canada through the Canada Book Fund and the Government of Ontario through the Ontario Book Publishing Tax Credit.

LIBRARY AND ARCHIVES CANADA CATALOGUING IN PUBLICATION

Title: The Baudelaire fractal / Lisa Robertson.
Names: Robertson, Lisa, 1961- author.
Identifiers: Canadiana (print) 20190142235 | Canadiana (ebook) 20190142251 | ISBN 9781552453902 (softcover) | ISBN 9781770566033 (PDF) | ISBN 9781770566026 (EPUB)
Classification: LCC PS8585.O3217 B38 2020 | DDC C813/.54—dc23

The Baudelaire Fractal is available as an ebook: ISBN 978 1 77056 603 3 (PDF); ISBN 978 1 77056 602 6 (EPUB)

'I have insupportable nervous troubles, exactly like women.'

  – Baudelaire, in a letter to his mother

'In this domain, as in *Sartor Resartus*, it is the masked, the disguised, or the costumed which turns out to be the truth of the uncovered.'

  – Deleuze, *Difference and Repetition*

These things happened, but not as described.

FOREIGN

Raised from babydom into doubt, I'm as feminine as Rousseau. I, Hazel Brown, eldest daughter of a disappearing class, penniless neophyte stunned by the glamour of literature, tradeless, clueless, yet with considerable moral stamina and luck, left my family at seventeen to seek a way to live. It was the month of June in 1979. I was looking for Beauty. I didn't exactly care about art, I simply wanted not to be bored and to experience grace. So I thought I would write. No other future seemed preferable. Let me be clear: I did not want to admire life, I did not want to skim it; I wanted to swim in it. I judged that to do this, I had to leave, and to write. I wanted to speak the beautiful language of my time, but without paying.

I myself was not beautiful. Moody, angular, both dark and pale, of bad posture, for I was perpetually thrust forward as if rushing into time, awkward whilst being observed, a half-broken tooth in my reluctant smile, uncertain in manners, premature frown lines between my grey-green eyes, all of this magnified by an urgency with no recognizable context: comedic in short, in the mode of a physical comedy.

Prodigal, undisciplined, with an aptitude for melancholy, I left houses, cities, lovers, schools, hotels, and countries. I left with haste, or I left languidly. Also I was asked to leave. I left languages and jobs. Leaving made a velocity. I left garments, books, notebooks, and several good companions. Sometimes I left ideas.

After the leaving, then what? I suppose I would drift. I had no money and no particular plan. Cities exist; hotels exist; painting exists. Tailoring also, it exists, as anger exists, mascara exists, and melancholy, and coffee. I liked sentences and I liked thread. Reading surely and excessively exists; also, convivially, perfume and punctuation. I had a fantasy and my diary. I had my desire, with its audacity, its elasticity, and its amplitude. I carried a powder-blue manual Smith Corona typewriter in a homemade tapestry bag. I was eager, sloppy, vague. I wore odd garments. I carried no letter of introduction, and I knew no one. I was only a girl bookworm. I wasn't to stay. None of this troubled me much.

The nervous fluid of a city is similar to a grammar or an electric current. Loving and loathing, we circulate. I myself did not exist before bathing in this medium. Here I become a style of enunciation, a strategic misunderstanding, a linguistic funnel, a wedge in language. Here I thought I'd destroy my origin, or I did destroy it, by becoming the she-dandy I found in the margins of used paperbacks. What do I love? I love the elsewhere of moving clouds.

Reading unfolds like a game called 'I,' in public gardens in good weather, in a series of worn-down hotel rooms, in museums in winter, where 'I' is the composite figure who is going to write but hasn't yet. If I am not alone in these rooms, if I could be known, it would be by the skinny red-haired street singer, the secretary of Cologne in her ironical cast-off dress, the hard-shod horsegirls neighing in the dark apartment, by similarly hybrid she-strangers and foreigners, any girl with the combined rage of lassitude and complicity.

They are blazons. Cool threads of anger bind me to them. We cease to be human. We're neutral, desituated clouds. There is nothing left to fear. This realization is a vocation.

My name is Hazel Brown.

THE PORT

I awake in a hotel room. I hear gulls, the clinking and rocking of boats. I turn in the wide bed. The tightness and stiffness of the sheets feels pleasantly confining. In the first stirrings of thinking I discover within myself a strangeness – not a dislocation or a dissociation, but a freshening shimmer of sensual clarity shot through with strands of unmoored refusal and scorn. Beneath that, a slowly vibrating warp of erotic sadness. I abandon myself to this novel sensation. I open my eyes. Reader, I become him. Was that what I felt? No, I did not become him; I became what he wrote.

Do you sometimes at earliest waking observe yourself struggling towards a pronoun? Do you fleetingly, as if from a great distance, strain to recall who it is that breathes and turns? Do you ever wish to quit the daily comedy of transforming into the I-speaker without abandoning the wilderness of sensing? The sensation isn't morbid; it is ultimately disinterested. For me it's a familiar moment, boring and persistent and disappointing. Again one arrives at the threshold of this particular, straitening *I*. With a tiny wincing flourish one enters the wearisome contract, sets foot to planks. Daily the humiliation is almost forgotten, until it blooms again with the next waking. It is an embarrassing perception best stoically flicked aside, left unreported. With an obscure hesitation one steps into the day and its frame and its costume.

Between the puzzlement and its summary abandonment, between the folds of waking consciousness and their subsequent limitation, is a possible city. Solitude, hotels, aging, love, hormones, alcohol, illness – these drifting experiences open it a little. Sometimes prolonged reading holds it ajar. Another's style of consciousness inflects one's own; an odd syntactic manner, a texture of embellishment, pause. A new mode of rest. I can feel physiologically haunted by a style. It's why I read ideally, for the structured liberation from the personal, yet the impersonal inflection can persist outside the text, beyond the passion of readerly empathy, a most satisfying transgression that arrives only inadvertently, never by force of intention. As if seized by a fateful kinship, against all the odds of sociology, the reader psychically assumes the cadence of the text. She sheds herself. This description tends towards a psychological interpretation of linguistics, but the experience is also spatial. I used to drive home from my lover's apartment at 2 a.m., 3 a.m. This was Vancouver in 1995. A zone of light-industrial neglect separated our two neighbourhoods. Between them the stretched-out city felt abandoned. My residual excitement and relaxation would extend outwards from my body and the speeding car, towards the dilapidated warehouses, the shut storefronts, the distant container yards, the dark exercise studios, the pools of sulphur light, towards a low-key dereliction. I would feel pretty much free. I was a driver, not a pronoun, not a being with breasts and anguish. I was neither with the lover nor alone. I was suspended in a nonchalance. My cells were at ease. I doted on nothing.

Now, after a long absence, I had returned to Vancouver as a visitor. I had delivered the lecture on wandering, tailoring, idleness, and doubt. I had conversed, feasted, slept. The following morning, alone in the hotel, I awoke to the bodily recognition that I had become the author of the complete works of Baudelaire. Even the unwritten texts, the notes and sketches contemplated and set aside, and also all of the correspondence, the fizzles and false starts and abandoned verses, the diaristic notes: I wrote them. Perhaps it is more precise to say that all at once, unbidden, I received the Baudelairean authorship, or that I found it within myself. This is obviously very different from being Baudelaire, which was not the case, nor my experience. I had only written his works.

It was a very quiet, neutral sensation. I associate it now with the observation of the immaterial precision of light.

Such an admission will seem frivolous, overdetermined, baroque. But I will venture this: it is no more singular for me to discover that I have written the complete works of Baudelaire than it was for me to have become a poet, me, a girl, in 1984. I was as if concussed. Believe me if you wish. I understand servitude. My task now is to fully serve this delusion.

Delusion needs an architecture; this hotel room became for a crucial instant the portal for a transmission seeking a conduit. Garments, rooms, paintings, desire: in each of these perceptual frames, there is the feeling of the movement of time as an inner experience made available to sensing and the wilderness of interpretation by way of material borders or limits. Time is my body, and it is also others' bodies; it could next become sentences, and the reflexive pause within the phrase. This is grace, I think: the achievement, in the company of strangers, of the necessary precision of the pause. A sentence flourishes only as a pause in thought, which extends the invitation of an identification. The great amateurs of fashion understand this supple grace. Garments can translate a city, map a previously unimagined mode of freedom or consent. A garment is a pause in textile. The pause admits untimeliness. One part of time acts counter to the will; one part of our bodily life is always and only untimely. We enter the room at precisely the wrong moment; we trip against the furniture, bruising our hips; we wake in the morning unable to recognize a suitable pronoun among the conventional phonemes. The garment must dress our untimeliness. I'm looking for the nonchalance expressed in an oddly shaped collar, a collar that appears to want to lift in the breeze of an open window to caress the line of my jaw. I'm intimate with the clumsy humour of buttons, the way a new kind of fit in a tailored jacket lifts my kidneys a little, coaxing open a readerly concave chest. At night the girls in galleries suddenly wear bright fringed shawls that move when they laugh, with hair slashed straight and high across their brows. There's a new textile, it seems, something from sports or a futuristic movie. It's lightweight and silvery, and the kids have plucked it off the internet to wear on the bus. It's being held to their skinny bodies by their heavy backpacks and the home-tattooed arms they slide across one another's waists. There's the erotic shimmer of a silk-thin band T-shirt on breast skin. The emotional synchrony of garments transmits discontinuously and by energetic means, thus the metaphysical appeal of fashion. I had studied this question of fashion's intellectual spirit in some of its great theorists – Lilly Reich, for example, and Rei Kawakubo – but also in my relationships to garments of every provenance. They need not have value in the commercial sense. There are the cast-offs and rejects, on eBay, in charity shops, draped over fences in modest residential alleys, swagging the rims of dumpsters by the apartment blocks, and certainly I have been a passionate amateur of their study and occasional acquisition. But here I'm not talking about the material research, as all-absorbing as it can become in its gradual, irregular advancement, but the mood of a garment, the way an emotional tone is brought forward in the wearing, in the suggestive affinities of the toilette. The unfamiliar set of a shoulder or the tugging sensation of a row of tight wrist buttons can hint at the gestural vocabulary of a previous epoch and so substitute for eroded or disappeared sentimental mores. Time in the garment is what I repeatedly sought, because sartorial time isn't singular but carries the living desires of bodies otherwise disappeared. This has been part of my perverse history of garment-love; I've wanted to inhabit the stances, gestures, and caresses of vanished passions and disciplines. And the various garments each person gathers to wear together, the way she groups fibres, colours, eras, social codes, and cuts, this mysterious grammar speaks beyond the tangible and often-cited economies and their various political constraints. I keep a home-sewn pale yellow silk shantung jacket that I haven't worn for decades because it once matched the hair of the girl who became my grandmother. I discovered this the season I myself was pale blonde, in 1983, the year of my grandmother's death. Garments are not signs in a signifying system, not in my cosmology. Fashion is the net of the history of love.

The hotel room was decorated with two prints of paintings, both seascapes. Around these portal-like rectangles the walls and fabrics were all placid tints of pale green and grey. It was curious that the decorator had taken such pains to establish an aquatic theme, given that Vancouver's own harbour was visible from the window. Yet these were not port images. They showed only unpeopled, unfigured planes of sky and sea, rendered in watercolour with some expertise, bisected or linked by their horizons. This now-tasteful minimalism of the previous decade left a polite space for reverie, as did the furnishings. I can't recall the carpet. It was Poe who said that the soul of an apartment is its carpet, and by this measure, I have rarely occupied a hotel room that could be said to have a soul. But I am not sure that I want a hotel room to have a soul, since the task of that innocuous limbo is to shelter mine, and unimagined others', with as few contradictions as possible. I go to the hotel to evade determination. What I thought of, what I imagined in this blandly contrived place as I woke, were those marvellously glowing baroque harbours by Claude Lorrain, the ones hanging in the Louvre. Listening to the boat sounds from my bed, watching the pale light slide in from beneath the sage-tinted curtain, I pictured the tall porticos rising on both sides of the sheltered water, pale columns rhyming with masts, the cheerful flapping of faded flags, the wooden hull of a great ship discharging cattle and wrapped bundles by means of little boats, bare-chested stevedores straining at their work while others, in red-and-blue belted tunics and matching turbans, stand by and discuss serious matters: impending weather conditions or import duties or the precarity of love. A cow in a sky-blue harness is being led by a man in a loin-cloth across a narrow gangplank to shore. I still keep an old postcard of this image, now bleached of its warm tones after being propped for several years on a sunny window ledge, so that my imagination of Claude has transmuted to cool-grey-green-blue, like the veiled marine sun of the Pacific port I now woke to. The more the Claude postcard fades, the more it resembles what I know.

The two imaginary seaports by Claude, these complex frontiers of an urban ambiance, as Guy Debord described them, were rivalled in their beauty, he said, by the Paris metro maps conveniently posted at stations. The affinity of the maps and Claude's seaports had to do, he claimed, with his char-acteristically utopian vagueness, with 'a sum of possibilities' rather than any compositional aesthetics. It's a literary mode of comparison, using not signs as its components, but the transformative potency of transitions. Metaphors, in other words. His method also takes into account the *anticipation* of transitions, not only the events themselves, which is what I like about metaphor, and about Debord: time is perversely multiplied. Nothing replaces anything else; contradictory sensations acquire contingent truth. The baroque seaports of Claude Lorrain exist right now as *future* potentials. I would agree with Debord about the psychogeographic equivalence of the harbour's beauty with the modern transports, but with the proviso that the similarity holds only for the time *before* one has ever visited Paris, when the metro and its map is still a pittoresque novella by Queneau borrowed from a small-town library, or glimpsed in a scene in a film by Godard, the one for example where Anna Karina, her childish face and pulled-back hair being lightly stroked all the while by her lover, looks at the presumed sadness of the other metro passengers – the moody boy with the cake box, the bored businessman reading the newspaper – and recites, then sings aloud, a poem by Aragon: *Things are what they are. From time to time the earth trembles.* The train pulls up to a station called Liberté. But is there a station called Liberty? I have never noticed it on any line I've travelled. And were the men sad? Maybe they were just angry. The tautly inflected instant of transformation between vocal recital and song, the poignant artifice of the threshold marked by a slight catch in her voice, a kind of physiological caesura or inflation that also seems spiritual, is what I recall most intensely of this film, first seen on a small static-strewn television screen in one of the shared sprawling apartments of the eighties, those roughly furnished places now mythic for their three-day parties and cut-up poems strewn across patterned blue carpets, also faded. Those carpets had soul – the pile rubbed bare to the rough jute warp in places of passage, the arabesque, as Poe called it, not only traced out in gridded botanical curlicues by the yarn of the pile, but stamped directly onto the now-visible jute backing with a kind of indelible blue-black ink. True, Poe preferred crimson carpets.

Transposed maps of different regions would be a variant explanation. The Vancouver hotel room I occupied that morning seemed in my state of half-wakefulness to contain all the hotel rooms and temporary rooms I had ever stayed in, not in a simultaneous continuum, nor in chronological sequence, but in flickering, overlapping, and partial surges, much in the way that a dream will dissolve into a new dream yet retain some colour or fragment of the previous dream, which across the pulsing transition both remains the same and plays a new role in an altered story, like a psychic rhyme, or a printed fabric whose complex pattern is built up across successive layers of impression, each autonomously perceptible but also leading the perceiver to cognitively connect the component parts in an inner act of fictive embellishment, so strong is the desire to recognize a narrative among scattered fragments of perception. My own youth seems to move in my present life in such a way – present and absent, at times incoherent, sometimes frightening, scarcely recognizable, rhyming and drifting.

I'm writing this in 2016 in a rented cottage at the edge of fields in central France. My task is to re-enter, by means of sentences, the course of my early apprenticeship. The desire to make a representative document began only with the involuntary incident in the hotel, the authorship that arrived both gradually and all at once. For a long time I have been more or less content with arcane researches that lead me into lush but impersonal lyric. Now I feel I must account for this anachronistic event; I'll follow it back to unspoken things. I want to make a story about the total implausibility of girlhood. This morning I'm at the round table under the linden tree, in a sweet green helmet of buzzing. Each of its pendulous flowers seems to be inhabited by a bee. They don't mind me – they're rapturously sucking nectar. I'm at the core of a breezy chandelier of honey. I'm sitting beneath the linden tree holding at bay the skepticism of my calling, describing how all at once, in a hotel by a harbour, I was seized by a kinship; how very slowly, in a weaving between cities and rooms, I became what I am not. Time has a style the way bodies do. There are turns and figures of iteration and relationship. But also times and bodies overlap. This work must annotate those parts of experience that evade determination. Here my fidelity is for the antithetical nature of the feminine concept. I was a girl. I could not escape desire, but now I can turn to contemplate it, and so convert my own complicity into writing. In this landscape time is pliable; it's a place of nightingales and poorness and wild cherry trees. Spring comes, slow and sudden. I'll work with that. I'll make this account using my nerves and my sentiment.

I'm writing this story backwards, from a shack in middle age. I sit and wait for as long as it takes until I intuit the shape of a sentence. Sometimes I feel that it is the room that writes. But it needs the hot nib of my pronoun.

In the cold autumn of 1984, when I was twenty-three years old, I decided to change my life. I flew from Vancouver to London with the plan to seek a new citizenship, continue to Paris, settle, and look for work. I carried one overpacked rip-stop nylon duffle bag, a sheaf of documents, and my type-writer. I found a hotel room near Victoria Station in what purported to be a Polish veterans' hostel, or that is what the sign said, where the cheapest of the remaining rooms, at eight pounds a night, was in the basement, with the word *Storage* written over the door. Perhaps the proprietor referred to it as the garden level. I did not mind because beside it was the bathroom, which had a very deep and long bathtub and a good supply of hot water, making it the warmest place in London that cold month. This bath was the antidote to the chilly museums where I passed my days sketching and writing in my diary, and my vain meanderings in Bloomsbury in search of the tea room where H.D. transformed herself to an Imagist in 1912. The second and important richness of the room, beyond its proximity to the bath, was the breakfast brought singingly to my door each morning by the Polish hotelman. Incredulous, I listed the contents of that tray in my diary: a tall glass of orange juice, a mug of very hot coffee, a demitasse of milk, a bowl of sugar, two eggs perfectly boiled, two slices of ham, a glass of marmalade, a plate with four slices of buttered brown bread and half a baguette, a tinfoil-wrapped candy, four chocolate lady's fingers, and a piece of cream-filled cake. So I would put three pieces of brown bread and all the sweets aside for my supper, returning from my day's wanderings with some cheese and lettuce to make sand-wiches. He would place the tray each morning on a small table covered with a yellow plasticized cabbage-rose-patterned cloth, which oddly matched the room's small hooked carpet, yellow also, dingy, and incongruously orna-mented with a brown cartoon bear. The wooden stand beside the narrow blue metal bed held a crucifix, a King James Bible, a spool of blue thread with a needle ready in it, and a 22p stamp. There also I kept the few books I travelled with – used paperback copies of Ezra Pound's *ABC of Reading*, Martin Heidegger's *Poetry, Language, Thought*, Sylvia Plath's *Winter Trees*, and a beautifully bound volume of Beat translations of classical Chinese poetry called *Old Friend from Far Away*. Why these books? Chance, I suppose. I was ardent and inex-perienced in my reading, earnestly drawing up lists of neces-sary future studies at the back of my diary, and as I read I seemed to float above the difficult and clever pages, in a haze of worshipful incomprehension. I imagined that simple persistence would slowly transform this vagueness to the hoped-for intelligent acuity, and in a way I was not wrong, although it was not true acuity that I later entered into, but the gradual ability, similar to the learning of a new handcraft, to perceive the threads linking book to book, and so to enter, through reading, a network of relationship. I might call this my education; save my gambits in parks and museums, I had had no other. Later this network would become an irritant, like a too-tight jacket, a binding collar. To counter this sad diminishment in my credulity, and to enter again the pleasurable drift, the sensual plenum of my youth, where even incomprehension was mildly erotic, in my middle age here in the cottage I have started to read French. I began with high-brow pornography, developing a taste for Pauline Réage, and eventually I moved from pornography to linguistics, and thence to poetry, led by Émile Benveniste and his theories of rhythm and semantics, to the works of Baudelaire. I was stunned by the sheer elegance of Benveniste's thought and puzzled by his absence from the North American canons. He led me to a fresh thinking of the movement of meaning in poetry; I abandoned the cult of the sign. I have had absolutely no irritating institutional knowledge to trouble my French reading, which is necessarily very partial and flawed. But I have with time lost the immature sense of self-incapacity, so useful in my earlier studies as a disciplining constraint. Always there would be something else that needed to be consulted before I could understand the book in hand. Always my path to that other text was slow, dependent on chance, libraries, and time-consuming love affairs. By the time I had laboriously located the errant reference, my own position had shifted. So my self-education took on an unintentional rigour. Now, with gusto, in the other language, I enter the cavalier abandonment of effortfulness.

I slept in that dark room in London for several weeks as I waited to procure a British passport. I had learned that I was eligible for this identity thanks to the accident of my father's birth in London. I am aware of how implausible this seems from the perspective of contemporary politics, but in 1984, with the appropriate paperwork in hand, a Canadian daughter of a British-born father could expect to receive British citizenship in under three weeks. Just before the Second World War, my paternal grandfather, a young radio genius fresh from the Saskatchewan farm, had travelled to England from Canada with his new wife to take a job in early radar technology. My grandmother had told me that she arrived in England already pregnant, continuously seasick during the Atlantic crossing on the empty coal freighter in which she and her economical husband had narrow wooden berths. Could that be so? I recall her telling me that when the empty ship docked in Liverpool, they had had to disembark by way of a flexible ladder thrown down the side of the steel hull from the high-riding deck, and when she arrived on the dock, the front of her new pastel-coloured travelling suit was deeply soiled. My grandmother was proud and precariously fashionable; this image hurt us both. They made their way from the entry port to the capital. And so my father was born to his young Canadian mother in a suburb of London, and so I visited this city nearly fifty years later to make claims to my identity, by means of various paper documents proving my father's birth, my parents' marriage, and my own legitimate, fully breach birth in Toronto during the crisis of the Bay of Pigs. I make the point regarding legitimacy since that was the purpose of the paperwork I presented to a woman in a cubicle of the passport office late one afternoon – to show the administrative traces of a patrilineal thread of blood linking me to this inhospitable island. When asked during the perfunctory interview, I had explained that I was applying for my British citizenship in order to live in France, and that I urgently wished to leave Britain. She didn't seem to mind. I received my new identity.

WINDOWS

It was at Paris on the first of November; I had embarked on the tour mandatory in the subtler education of any worthy young man, two centuries previous. But I was a girl in 1984. Always I was to be askew, belated. I arrived by train very early in the morning and the hotels were not yet open in the Latin Quarter. Madonna was on all the kiosk posters. I preferred Gena Rowlands, or Fanny Ardant. The aproned waiter poured the little jug of hot milk into the coffee cup with a flourish, at the table. In the parks and squares the chestnuts were splitting their green cases. The air was sharp and tannic. This was the city I had invented for myself by reading. I had an address scribbled on the last page of my journal: *52 rue Gay-Lussac – Hotel Avenir*.

How will I explain the taste and aroma of slightly overripe Mirabelle plums? I am eating a chilled dish of them now beneath the linden as I recollect that first room in Paris. I was a girl because I had not yet decided on my destiny. But I had recognized something about its setting. Now I under-stand that I was haunted by the problematic ratios of sex and art, of anger and sadness. I've never solved them. My researches then lacked consistency and were too literal. I would sit on trains and write in my hardback journal about the mythologization of maternity in relation to the frustrated inner feeling of calling or ambition (intuitively, I'd rather have had a calling than an ambition; ambitious girls were cruelly judged) as I permitted my ankle to brush and linger next the caressing ankle of the sullen boy sitting across from me in the second-class compartment. I would seek cheap city rooms in order to look out from their windows at unfamiliar surface effects and the shade the angles made. Having a soul, I thought, is about looking out. I would look out, and then write again in my diary. I exoticized Old World neglect. I was looking for a neutral place where my ambition might ripen, unhampered by scorn. Such a room could be found in the Hotel Avenir for seventy francs a night, or twelve dollars Canadian, in the currency of the time, which had the satisfying merit of being payable entirely in thick, brassy ten-franc coins.

Steve Lacy's horn cuts lingeringly across a tannic landscape. I'm listening to *Monk's Dream*. The cold sweet plums carry the smallest possible hint of musky leather. The toughened skin gives a little beneath the teeth before it bursts to a boozy exuberance. I've reopened the old journals.

Baudelaire said art must be stupid. I know what he means. Art must be as stupid as a plum. As stupid as an ankle.

In that first hotel in Paris, a previously respectable but by then faded establishment near the Luxembourg Gardens and the boulevard Saint-Michel, a place I would later recognize in a documentary photograph of the burnt-out cars near the boulevard in the month of May 1968, the narrow room on the fifth floor was reached by a frail elevator used only by guests, never by the tired hostess. Each morning she would descend the steep staircase entirely obscured by a rumpled mound of used sheets. Mine was the cheapest, smallest room, which in Paris would always be on the top floor. The cotlike bed presented a challenging topography; I would shift my skinny hips to seek the sweet place between the wadded mattress lumps. At the foot of the bed was a narrow table, and above the table a window looked into the dim inner court. Street views were more expensive. This shady window communicated with a facing window of the hotel or apartment house that shared a shaded inner ventilation well used by the concierges to air their mops and rags. In keeping with the hotel's convention, I call it a court, but with no grandeur. It was more properly speaking a chute, or a more spacious than usual vent. The air of this inner court was sealike.

Through this window, across the humid court, I saw a boy sitting also at his own table, a dark-haired boy in a white shirt turned turquoise by the dim light, bent a little at his typewriter.

Of all stupid art the poem is the most stupid, a nearly imperceptible flick of the mop just beneath the surface of the water, an idle flutter of the hand. Very stupid; outside all good sense and discretion, because the poem must be indiscreet or not at all. It should just trail aimlessly in the hospitable water. Floating on the sea or swimming. It must be the sea, no other water. Waves, but not stormy waves, the slight rocking movement. This floating is like a hotel. Nothing interrupts sensation; the body is supported and welcomed by a gentle neutrality. Especially the sea on an overcast morning of light rain, the encompassing pleasure enveloping the skin, salt water and soft water, I will take a bath, I will write all morning in a hotel, I will lack nothing, the soft coarse sheets wind around me, I float in the possibility of drifting unattended, the freedom of floating, no weight, no companion, just the hospitality of the encompassing element. A slight coolness is enough to bring the attention to the sensation of water on skin, of worn cotton on skin. Or perhaps in a café in the village in summer, the bells ringing, the irregular waves of conversation, occasional scraping of chairs on stone pavement, but mostly floating, in the sea or in a hotel. The superior hospitality of the threadbare hotel, the minimal frisson of slight discomfort, as in cool water, which augments the feeling of the skin, the feeling of being only skin, punctuates the sensation of being in the minimum calmly, as in an element. The elemental hospitality of the inferior hotel, felt in the minimal, even ironical welcome, the absence of any exaggeration or luxury that would leave one in its debt, the muteness and reluctance of the clerk: this is the stupidity I crave.

In the communicating window close across the dim court, adrift also in the hospitable element, not glancing upward from his heavy black book, his serious typewriter mirroring my own, the image of the studious youth seated at his writing composed itself in my self-image. Only this morning, eating plums, consulting that old diary, which by a peculiar fate I have preserved all these decades since, do I rediscover that the first hotel was called the Future. I know that he also looked outwards across the court to notice me sitting at the foot of the bed to work at my own table, frowning over my Penguin Classic, writing in the brown leather-bound and marbled volume, too heavy, too formal, too contrived for my cheap nylon travelling satchel: belated, nineteenth-century. I know this because I received his gaze and returned it. This exchange would slowly ripen in me, tenacious, voluble, through all the travels that were to follow, the movements between and within cities, from hotels to museums and libraries, from table to bath. Eventually, through a clandestine but thorough metamorphosis of my sentiments, the mutual gaze of the inner court at the Hotel Avenir would transmute within me to become the concussive authorship.

Time in water is pliable. The greenish mop scent drifting upwards weedlike, the boatlike creaking of the wooden shutters, the liquidity of the smoke of the Baudelairean boy with his sharp, aquiline nose and close-cropped dark hair across the court in the communicating window, the quivering shadow and refracted light: in fact, the inside court was a sea in the way it combined so many separate things in a subtly swirling, rocking motion to make of them a single encompassing element. The shared gaze through the humid court inaugurated in me a series of concepts I could not at that time fully recognize, with my lazy habits, my vague tendency to drift only on the substance of another's desire, desire found in the lazily skimmed pages of books, the desire of a boy in gardens or on boulevards or on stairwells or in seminars as I clasped my Penguin Nietzsche, worn soft by incomprehension.

I had received the image of the Baudelairean boy through the medium of the moppish air of the hotel of the future's inner court. Such is a girl's destiny, this scant enclosure of fumy potential that later will reveal itself as the elemental core of her life. She will sit at tables eating overripe plums and burning incense, frowning a little, her sleeves rolled – no, her jacket unbuttoned at the top to show the saffron-coloured neckscarf. The narrow grey inner court of the future hotel will have become her sealike matrix.

When Courbet painted the young poet reading at his work table in 1848, the year of the Revolution so acerbically caricatured in Flaubert's *Sentimental Education*, the year the boy gesticulated with a revolver on a street corner calling for the assassination of his stepfather the Colonel Aupick, the year of his first translation of Edgar Allan Poe, Baudelaire, in his moment of socialism, having just lost his inheritance, was living on rue de Babylone in the 7th arrondissement, perhaps in the room of his mistress, Jeanne Duval. This was one of a long series of rooms, either hotel rooms or borrowed apartments, occupied for varying brief periods from the age of twenty-three, when his family had seized his fortune by court order, then doled it back to him through their notary in direly inadequate monthly increments, until his death at forty-six. After a brief period of luxurious and extreme expenditure – garments for his mistresses and for himself, baroque furnishings and draperies, perfumes, wines, hashish, and antique paintings, most of which later proved to be forgeries – his scandalized bourgeois family had him declared a legal minor by the courts. From this moment until the end of his life, he lost all the legal and financial rights of his majority. He could not own, nor vote, nor marry. The poet spent twenty-three years of his life actively fleeing creditors, working clandestinely, moving on in the night, often assisted by Jeanne Duval. I am astounded that under these extreme conditions he was able to write anything. Here in Courbet's portrait he seems to be sitting on a carmine-coloured divan and is wearing a matching lap rug. A bare wooden table is pulled close to balance on its lip the open weight of the thick black volume that the young man, pipe in mouth, is reading with intense focus. He is smoking. Two other books are stacked on a ribbon-tied dark green mottled cardboard folder of the kind still available in most French stationers' shops, and as part of this studious still life, a long feather pen slashes diagonally, palely upwards from the inkwell into the putty-toned shadow. The opaque plume has captured the late slant of light; so has the creamy splayed deckle edge of the open book. Similarly lit is the poet's delicate left hand, resting at his side, expressive even in its immobility. I recall the Goncourt brothers, in their journals, mentioning glimpsing Baudelaire some ten years later in the Café Riche, a stylish place for publishers and the last regency drunks, as they said. It was shortly after the damning 1857 obscenity trial of *Les Fleurs du mal*: 'his shirt open at the neck and his head shaved, just as if he were going to be guillotined. A single affectation: his little hands washed and cared for, the nails kept scrupulously clean, like a woman.' The two judgments, one against his legal majority and one against his book, determined the form of the poet's adult life.

His fine hands, one quizzically posed beneath his chin, chin decorated with a little quirky beard, beard worn as a self-amused form of punctuation, the other hand delicately worrying the carved arm of the ornate wooden armchair in which he was seated, also occupy the foreground of the earlier, and only other portrait, by Émile Deroy. This youthful likeness, which his friend Asselineau described as hanging in the poet's apartment during his early period of luxury at the Hotel Pimodan, followed him through the long itinerancy of rented rooms that Baudelaire struggled to wear lightly in his later years. Deroy had made the painting over three nights, in lamplight, in Baudelaire's salon, in the company of the poet Théodore de Banville, who later described the scene in his memoirs, the Guadeloupian Creole journalist Alexandre Privat d'Anglemont, and the Lyonais socialist songwriter Pierre Dupont, the five young men, inseparable then, smoking and talking about Delacroix and the tensions between colour and line, verse and girls.

But for now I want to return to the story of Courbet, who was to show his own portrait of Baudelaire in 1855 along with forty other of his own works in a rented hangar-like wooden building, as part of a flamboyantly rebellious exhibition of his own devising called *The Pavilion of Realism*. Though the artist had previously enjoyed considerable success with his portraits, his monumental painting *The Artist's Studio: A Real Allegory Summing Up Seven Years of My Artistic and Moral Life* was rejected by the jury of the Exposition Universelle. He responded to this rejection with enthusiasm, borrowing money from a collector to fund a temporary exhibition hall of his own. Initially imagined in his correspondence as a circus tent, it stood next to the exhibition hall of the prestigious and well-visited Exposition Universelle. *The Pavilion of Realism* was a large-scale work of hubristic publicity. Courbet converted the long exterior wall of the building into a billboard advertising his name; you paid a nominal entrance fee, the first time such fees had been charged to exhibition visitors in France, and you also paid to leave your umbrella or walking stick with an attendant, to purchase a souvenir photographic image of the rejected tableau, or to take an exhibition catalogue, within which was printed Courbet's own text 'The Manifesto of Realism.' 'I simply wanted to draw forth, from a complete acquaintance with tradition, the reasoned and independent consciousness of my own individuality,' he wrote, defending the painting as a depiction of the present as a synthetic vision of the people he saw and dealt with daily in the city, people of various social classes and fortunes. He had been influenced by Baudelaire who, in his Salon of 1846, had first addressed the topic of the necessary relationship of art to urban modernity. Beauty, Baudelaire wrote in his Salon, was the beauty of the present only, and was necessarily composed of elements both absolute and quotidian, whose association caused the sensation of marvellousness, which is modern. Each age, each milieu, has its own beauty, as it has its fashions, elegance, debaucheries, and vileness. Each age has its own violence and injustice. All of this flickering together is what the new artist must represent. Beauty was only ever modern, in modernity's costumes, said Baudelaire. It would not be dressed in classical robes and attitudes; the new beauty would be found in the daily life of the city, in its real mixtures and extremes. Already we live amidst beauty but we do not recognize it, he said. In his allegorical studio, Courbet had depicted the poet half-seated on a wooden table in the lower right-hand corner, bent over a large open book whose pages provide one of the few instances of intense light in a painting modelled according to a profound, almost baroque chiaroscuro.

Influenced by his interpretation of Baudelairean realism, Courbet depicted himself in the centre of his crowded studio, painting a scenic landscape at his easel. Behind him, a naked white woman, plump, half-turned from the viewer, holds up some drapery to cover her breast, and watches the painter work. Her pale pink garments lie crumpled at their feet in the foreground, like an oversweet dessert. She is his model, but not for this image. On the left of the artist, in the darkest shadow, is a motley grouping of people from all parts of life: actors, a money lender, a clothier, a lactating Irish peasant woman with infant, musicians, an acrobat, a priest, a Christ figure, a radical, a farmer, and a standing boy, respectfully watching him paint. To Courbet's right is a second group, his peers: intellectuals, critics, politicians, gallerists and their wives, all of them fashionably clothed – the men in dark suits, the woman closest to us in an opulently embroidered shawl. A child plays with a cat at the feet of the adults; he is drawing his own picture on a large sheet of paper laid flat on the floor. The figures in this modern allegory all float across the thickly painted darkness as if projected in a film. The artist, in the centre, is the hero of his drama or diorama. Baudelaire's figure is set apart from the others; he is absorbed in his reading, apparently alone.

When I arrived in Paris, my own experience of the life of an artist's studio was limited to a memory of my grand-mother's paint-scented spare room, in her little postwar house in North Toronto, where she left her easel set up at the foot of the tidily made bed. Her diminutive canvases – 'oils,' as she called them – depicted the abandoned farmhouses and ruined barns and silos of Southern Ontario, in her tastefully muted palette of greyed-down greens and silvery taupes. Thus the colonial remnants of Kantian sublimity came to perch on an old lady's easel in my grandmother's spare room of a modest bungalow in suburban Toronto in 1971. I adored this room, its scent and mysterious equipment. I learned there that when I stood in front of paintings, I could feel an inner vibration. It entered flatly through the entire surface of my body if I let myself go blank. In my adolescent movements from my grandmother's guest room to provincial art museums, I came to think of the mute mineral affinity that accompanied my blankness as a psychic life of pigment. In front of paintings, my body had autonomous gifts, useful only to my own inner experience. This pigment-sense didn't have anything to do with representation or style, yet it was dependent on the proportions and specificities of mixture. I think my feeling for painting is a deferred material telepathy, an elemental magnetism. I was noticing a mineral sympathy of my body's iron and copper and calcium towards paint. I learned to still myself to make room for this strange reception. In the spare room, I first came to the recognition that I could be changed by these little documents of admixture, through the simple attention of a slowed, non-linguistic perceiving. The change had to do with the deepening sensation of interior space by means of immaterial correspondences. Pigment striates the subject. Mineral affinities act within and across bodies and across times. We are paintings.

It is evident that the image of Baudelaire in Courbet's studio allegory has been transposed from the earlier portrait: the oblique light, the studious posture, the curve of the stooped shoulder link the two representations. In *The Artist's Studio*, the entire crowded and mysterious image, so inclusive in its social cosmology, seems to radiate out and across the canvas from the dark lower-corner figure of Baudelaire bent over his books. One book is open; on another closed volume rests the poet's nervous hand. The energy inaugurated in the earlier portrait by the placement of that tentative and nervous hand leads us to believe that at any instant Baudelaire will pause in his reading in order to reach for the splendid quill.

When I began to write I trembled with an almost immediately disappointed ambition, but I liked paper and I liked ink. This much has remained constant or at least recurrent. The ambition had to do with a hoped-for intimacy between sentences and sensation. I believed that my future was located in the flagrant interstices of this relation, that an architecture capable of welcoming my essential nudity would reveal itself on the threshold of the page. I had no worldly knowledge and no aspirations towards anything that might be termed a literary society. I did not then suspect that such a society existed in the present; if it did, I was ignorant of any access to it. I needed to write in order to make a site for my body. There would be no other way to uncover my unwieldy desire. I was learning that the social fiasco of sex was not a reliable method. So many bludgeoning projections, such petty incompetence and scorn, so many mythological charades worked to lessen the mere possibility of sensual amplitude. I would never understand sex. I could not be that thing and learn to appear to myself. Sadness always undermined the pleasure. So I decided to understand sentences. There would be detours. My own allegorical studio then contained only my typewriter, the diaries, some books, and the figures I found in them. But I was always beginning to write. On every page of the heavy marbled journal I began, heavy with stupidity. The grand tradition had dissolved and the new one hadn't yet been made. How girlish his hand. How fresh the feather looked.

ANYWHERE OUT OF THE WORLD

Here in the story I would go to kiss in a park all afternoon because that was the luxury I preferred, to kiss a nameless boy near fountains, then return alone to my bare hotel. It was a critical act, it was studied and researched and questioned, and it was personal. Also, delicious. I imagined that I was a part of a *fête galante* by Watteau, *Pilgrimage to Cythera* for example, my adventures all overhung by sensuous masses of foliage. I had not yet been exposed to the fashion that would later become so attractive to me, the craze for transforming each experience into a concept. I had just my existence and my will and something like a calling, and this didn't trouble me, and it didn't burden my critique. I was a girl, and my body was time. I believed in description. I would build new, ornate knowledge on the basis of this lived proposition. I mean that my shy, gawky, lusting body was constrained to undertake the ancient representation, to groom and flirt and refract as every contemporary girl seemed so constrained, to signify bounty and frailty, passivity and fate, but also at this time there was the fact that I loosely accepted the constraint. It taught me something about discipline and a lot about a history of form. Form meant my mutable body. Form could even weep. My own interpretation of the form of life of girlhood would rakishly embellish a margin of moody nonchalance, much as a pianist, whilst perched on a diminutive stool, hums a little during their slowed-down interpretation of Bach.

To visit those fountains, I preferred to wear outmoded garments that fit poorly, garments mended or taken in with large stitches or barely hidden safety pins, or lacking a sewing kit, perchance paperclips, and I liked lugubrious coats with ample hems and the wrong cut of shoulder, the fastidiously dated lapel, the cheaply glittering brooch, the long string of chipped green glass beads. I would be the girl of my notion of literature, or rather my invention of literature, since, still lacking any concept, I could only invent. My outfits and their compositions were experiments in syntax and diction. So, much as later, in a different life, I would submit my poems to collective tables and risk embarrassed exposure, with defiant awkwardness I would take my sartorial representations to the parks and boulevards, and I would kiss, then back in my room I would write little essays, such as:

ESSAY ON THE IMAGINATION

In the green shade the bird is green.
Every night has a goat in it, and a peacock and a dove.

No, that is morning.

While a man in a hotel is in a crematorium, or in the negative image of a church (I refer here to Walter Benjamin and Siegfried Kracauer's melancholic theorizations), a girl in her hotel is free. I want to claim this word *free* for myself and I intend to use it wrongly very often. Here by free I mean that nothing is meant for her. She is outside history, outside poetry, outside theology, outside thought, outside money. Therefore she should claim anything: this was the fundamental recognition of my youthful travels. Freedom must be wrongly performed or it will be irrelevant. So I went to my hotel as Descartes withdrew to his Dutch chamber, in order to begin thought wrongly, to throw everything away because I wanted to begin.

You may wonder how I financed this endeavour. I gathered a sum of money working in Normandy as domestic companion to an elderly Huguenot widow of the Algerian War, a distant descendant of Baron Haussmann. *Jeune fille compagne* was the term. I knew very little history and certainly nothing of the Algerian War, which had not been mentioned in my mediocre education, a so-called education that had simply omitted any mention of the colonialism of the recent past. Many wars and even countries simply did not exist for me then. I was from a class that persisted in imagining that its own complacency was natural.

The widow, convalescing from hip surgery, and so requiring paid companionship, continued to wear her silver Berber bracelets, as she had since 1962, and they rattled when she gestured with her cane. This was Madame's summer house, the place where she entertained the nearby Protestant bourgeoisie, genteel families whose fortunes were long ago founded on wine, perfume, banking, and silk. All the women wore the gold cross of Malta on delicate chains, and these crosses would often become entangled with the chubby pearls that were the second component of their symbolic accessorization, the third being the perfume of Guerlain, the great nineteenth-century house. Each of these three feminine insignia was received as a gift and assumed at puberty. In this high-society pastoral, I cooked and sewed and weeded the mixed borders, but did not have to iron, since a sturdy middle-aged woman from the village came twice weekly to perform this rite, seemingly the hot core of household stability. We discussed the day's menus at the breakfast table, and sometimes Madame recounted stories of nighttime spiritual visions of white light. Evenings I politely served her guests. At these dinners, for obscure doctrinal reasons, I was forbidden to wear black or red, which presented me with a wardrobe conundrum, and so Madame gave me a length of cloying pink cotton piqué from which to sew my own uniform: a modest gathered skirt and matching blouse. Lapsed Toronto Protestant that I am, I executed the command obediently using a *Vogue* designer sewing pattern by Calvin Klein, then wore this docile costume to change the plates between courses. Seeing that I had a knack for textiles, she instructed me next to line her walnut armoires with cheerful printed cottons from the south. Beneath the hazelnut tree, as Madame embroidered bassinet skirts for her coming grandchild's layette – '*il faut que je finisse ce berceau … il faut que je finisse ce berceau …*' – or indoors in front of the televised Roland-Garros tennis championships, applauding Yannick Noah to the muted rhythm of thwacking balls and hushed applause, I received lessons in language, needlework, and domestic comportment. After several months of these textile instructions, my frustration mounting as I tried to type poems in rooms inevitably shared with visiting grandchildren, the summer ended, and, carrying a thick envelope of paper money and a copy of Barthes's *Fragments d'un discours amoureux* I had procured in Dieppe, I left.

How did I next live my freedom, beyond the mock-pastoral kissing? Looking back to that time is like the experience of glimpsing the incipient or dissolving activity at the borders of a room when you pass into it, an image dear to Pierre Bonnard, who painted the formal decadence of domesticity. 'I'm trying to do what I have never done,' said the painter of those homely, askew, and yet shimmering compositions, 'give the impression one has on entering a room: one sees everything and at the same time nothing.' But where Bonnard's thresholds are quivering with the dissolution of pattern, always about to be crossed by their spectral, colourfully dressed occupants, much as I, paid domestic companion, had bustled from task to task, a sort of thin, vigorously animated overpainting, what I entered now in my hotel was an annulment of arbitrary conduct and designation. Here I sensed the absence of the previous occupants, all of them strangers, and so featureless, and the absence functioned as a kind of invitation to the tedium of my own interior life, a tedium akin to the boredom or spacious featurelessness of the tidy yet dusty room. Featurelessness was what I craved. This room's spiritual flatness was a matrix. I did not share Benjamin's longing for the macabre bourgeois house, with its glossy large-leafed plants, its funereal slipcovers and curtains and carpets, all aired and cleaned and repaired twice annually, with its collections of porcelain, crowds of good family furniture, and scent of wax. It seemed to me that what Benjamin really pined for was the grotesque invisibility of the female work that maintained this mirage, whether purchased or married. I had fled that contract. The places I stayed in were not very clean, and that was fine. They did not pertain to the recognizably female narrative of domesticity I despised. The open question of my future, of what I was to become, felt smooth and shadowy, liberated by these rooms into a textile-like anonymity, patterned with light strokes of pigment and splashes of unaccountable shade.

The cool threshold vibrated with sparseness. Then the hotel's enclosed scent opened like a grove. I, a girl, exultant, crossed into the room of sentences. This room was suddenly ornate with the written vestiges of silence. No judgment, no need, no contract, no seduction: just the free promiscuity of a disrobed mind.

The room is everything that is the case. The room is everything that is time. It is entirely unexceptional. Each time, the room, this room. I fell upon it unexceptionally. I had been testing the limits exercised by the world upon my girlishness. In the world that deemed me girl, what could I do with pleasure? What could I do for pleasure? I could kiss, I could go to the library, I could study garments. I could explore the possible relationships among these three things. Several of the possible relationships or combinations were more or less interesting, for a while. In the room, though, there was a fourth thing, and a fifth. Entirely outside servitude, I could read and I could think, finally understanding the unexceptional character of these acts. Free of all personal particularity, I read and I thought. I will call it thought, though when I placed it beside the thought of the philosophers, which I unfolded improprietously from within the creased paperbacks, there was no likeness, no identity. I was not bothered. What I felt as thought was at least my own, I believed. The room was not the world, the world that deemed me thing, the world against which I continually bumped and scraped my awkward body as I attempted to move with guessed-at elegance. It was the other world. It is the case that I fell upon this other world of the room accidentally, as falls go. The room demanded no grace. It wanted nothing from me. I fell and then I dallied. The accident of this fall, which is to say, the sudden revelation of the unexceptional character of my soul, when otherwise I had been constrained to sense myself as feminine and so exceptional, and had churlishly accepted the worldly constraint, now introduced me to a more exacting constraint, the constraint of the basic and unexceptional realization of the neutrality, the indifference, the essentially dandiacal aspect of my soul.

The room was crowded at its edges with the written souls of strangers, and this was its particular comfort. I had no responsibilities towards those souls. I could fetch nothing for them. Neither their comfort nor their pleasure were my domain. They were there because I did not care for them perhaps. I did not need them to pay me anything.

Unaware of the thoroughly comedic nature of the situation, I continued to cross into such rooms, this room, the room of my unexceptional dalliance. I say unaware, but that is not the just word. Comedy was present but latent. The ironic burlesque of the girl reading, the girl lying diagonally across the bed, across the picture plane, this was a genre I had witnessed in the museums of my travels, and also the burlesque of the female reader's fingers inserted between the pages of the book as if to say here, only here, am I not. These gentle gestures, gestures that were barely actions – the fingers within the book, the pressure of my belly across the too-soft, bowing mattress, the dark fringe of my growing-out hair flopping repeatedly between my gaze and the book, the upward flex of my knees and the rhythmic movement of my bare foot as I turned a page – transformed me into an image of a reader. But far from limiting the possibilities of my inner experience, the little unthought movements made by my body, which from the point of view of an observer would designate me as image within a pictorial tradition, also brought me to the quiet certitude of this body, my odd body, as an image for thinking, an image for my own free use. Here sprung the comedy. Already my body was inside thought. The strangeness of the image, my body, the girl, her inescapable maladroitness – always leaking, bruising, stinking, lusting – originates the infraction that thought must be. For the girl is an infraction in thought. She simply needs to annotate the breach that she is as her reading destroys the purity of philosophy. The idea was hilarious, capacious, like the best burlesque. When in *An American in Paris* Gene Kelly wakes up in his shiplike room, a tiny space where every furnishing folds or unfolds to become something else, when he enters the elegantly improvised choreography of grooming and beginning his Parisian day, the habitual movements of his compact yet lanky frame unfolding for his own pleasure, like a philosopher's quotidian thought, but unfolding also with the gentle artifice of the awareness of being perceived, the charm of his dance being his simultaneous refusal of and dalliance with this artifice – were the table, the bed, the basin his perceivers? This was my sensation when I read. It was funny and it was to become contractual. Insofar as I, or rather my body, was an image, an image of the comedy of the girl in thought, I discovered an image to be a composite inner stance or posture. It wasn't a sign; its meaning was not fixed. The image was synthetic, made, and so mutating and potent. I was not a sign; therefore, I wasn't a woman either. The image was a fecund entanglement, an infraction that acted within the person, and between persons, and between eras also, a complex of memory, minerals, sensation, and lust. Everything that happened to me then lingered within me, latent, to next spontaneously transform the image of what I'm now saying. The reading girl, the soft action of her fingers in the text, will become philosophy, will become poetry, in a passive but total infiltration.

The glimpsed and evasive everythingness of Bonnard's pictures, the crowded but silently unprepossessing borders of the room, the skewed belatedness of perceiving, my desire to slip away, my metamorphosis inside the room to the image of the girl in thought: these are strands of memory. Not all of the image would reveal itself in the present. It was the appearance of a large brown spider in my basin today that returned me to this earlier room and the spider that had materialized one morning in its stained porcelain bowl. I would then, as now, cruelly permit the creature to live for several days as a mascot or a pet, carefully avoiding rinsing it away, adjusting and minimizing my grooming procedures so that I could continue to observe it, and it me. Outside the basin this spider would perhaps be dangerous. Who was I to know. It could not escape the slant porcelain world it had accidently appeared within, perhaps from up the sour drain, perhaps from above on its invisible thread. I felt, I feel, accompanied by this spider. If part of the image is for the future or already with the future, the image being, as I was discovering in my rooms, a synthesis or recomposition of time as well as of all kinds of sensation, resurging suddenly to stay awhile like a brown spider, if part of comedy is cruelty, what of the parts of the image that were to be forgotten? Where do the forgotten parts stay? Fragments of my sensation sequestered themselves within books, or in cheap rooms. Here I uncover them again.

Was this room in Avignon or was it in Marseilles? I am no longer certain. Any room near any fountain was paradise, so it hardly matters. The experience of time at the edges of rooms, at the edges of books, time disappearing or bending as I entered, this is my borderless image, the experience of the disappearance of the word at the appearance of the flower. I recall, for instance, an odd recent period when I forgot the word *asphodel*. The forgetting persisted for more than a week, the week in April, as it happened, when at the borders of the woods near my cottage the asphodel bloomed. I could both see and imagine the ranks of tall ghostly stalks, but the name was absent. And so I thought frequently about asphodels, systematically approaching the absence of the flower's name from each vantage possible, thinking of the opening lines of the beautiful late poem by William Carlos Williams, yet subtracted of the name, remembering the asphodel meadows that would emerge before blackberry vines, where the woods had been cut down for heating wood. 'A field made up of women / all silver-white.' At the margin of each room I enter are asphodels, womanly, at the instant they lose their name. This is a form of self-knowledge, a philosophy. The long period of my life between learning the word *asphodel* when first reading the Williams poem in the London hotel room, or had it been in a bookshop, just before closing – a ghost of a pressed flower had slipped out of the second-hand book, it was 1984 – and seeing the living flower for the first time only recently, walking in April with my elderly dog, recognizing the flower in the midst of the flicker of linguistic forgetting, this space so active and evacuating at its limits, so welcoming at its empty core, the entanglement of the name's absence with the striving and failing, the entanglement of gold chain and pearl, the fibs and embellishments and delusions and obfuscations: in the expanding work of forgetting the word *asphodel*, this flower so flagrantly inhabited the edge of every perception, every memory, that I thought perhaps I could know the name only when I did not know the flower, or only outside the brief season of its bloom, even outside the season of its black budding. I happened upon an emancipation from vocables into the substance of mortality. Slowly, obstinately, the room will be stripped of every conceptual dimension. Every word will be lost. Others will continue the kissing.

VOCATIONS

I remember the room as being quite high up in the ancient building, the building itself near the top of the Montagne Sainte-Geneviève. We climbed what felt like endless flights of dark stairs to get there, his solid back sweating lightly through the gleaming white shirt just a step above me, his hand softly trailing back to touch my fingers. As we climbed, my tenderness for the nameless boy kept expanding, tenderness for the closely cropped dark hair on the nape of his neck, for his sweat-mottled shirt, his acrid scent mixed with sweet soap, the soft trailing plantlike insistence of his trailing-back hand, my tenderness for the darkness of the shabby, steep stair, for the green park bench where I had been sitting with my Nietzsche, for the unread paperback in my satchel, now bouncing softly against my hip, for my own ordinariness in my loose corduroys and cheap tailored jacket and brown sandals, an ordinary girl now extraordinarily climbing a strange stair in mid-afternoon: susceptibility expanded continuously in my chest as I climbed so that I mistook it for desire, though I did then believe that it was desire that I felt. Internally, to myself, I said words like *passion*, and I believed in that gravitas. What was desire then and what is it now? A kind of poetry maybe. A body of poetry. The opposite of identity. What I wanted ardently was poetry, and to me this expansive afternoon felt like poetry ought to feel. The entire world, everything it would be possible for me to experience in my life, the anticipation of each kiss and its singularity and rhythm, each angular, difficult, sparkling philosophy, each impersonal room, rooms that would structure my thought and my ambitions, opened into our shadowy and eager ascent. Reader, I am still in that stairwell as I write this. I will never leave it. The splendid freedom of climbing the dark stair that curved above into unknowing, the light scent of dust and sweat and soap, my sensation of internal expansion, expectation mixed with strangeness, the receptivity of my skin augmented as if by a mystic cosmetic: I was then the expanse of what I felt in the limitless afternoon. There was no sadness attached to the anonymity of it, and no fear either. Since I couldn't then write the poems I wanted to write, I would be the poet of the anonymous fuck. This was not so much a substitution as a technique of self-invention, an experimental method for the grandness of becoming. Other poets, I would later learn, had mentors, whatever mentors were. I had fucking, and it was my own blind affirmation, my autonomy, my own urgent need to fully know the grand world. I felt possessive about it, not fearful. Not the boy himself, but the full world and his part of it. Tenderness, the internal detailed question opened by this desire to know everything. Poetry, its livid shape. It didn't need to be written yet. Maybe it was a bad poem, a bad fuck, but if that was so, it was very bad, gratingly, oppressively bad: there was nothing mediocre about it, nothing partial, nothing lacking.

We reached the top of the stair. Inside his door the abrupt light was shocking and I felt even more certain in my seeking tenderness. I still feel it so I slicken. He offered me whisky and I accepted. He was a kind, provincial boy with a bottle of Johnnie Walker in an unpretentious room. This room was clean and bare and had been recently painted a glossy pale yellow. It was small; the one window faced the very large inner court. I saw the tops of trees. The table, where we sat to drink, was pushed up beneath it in sunlight. There was a makeshift toilet cabin enclosed by a shower curtain, constructed in such a way that it awkwardly divided the space. Later I would shower there, at his invitation. Over the narrow bed in the back corner, two posters – one, Warhol's Marilyn; the other, a glittering skyline of New York by night. The boy had New World ambitions, but for the time being it wasn't clear to me what he was. Each month his father would laboriously climb these steps, bringing a large suitcase of clean laundry from the country and returning home on the train with the soiled in the same suitcase. I was willing to go to such rooms. But what can be known.

We had met in the Luxembourg Gardens at 3 p.m.; I had been sitting on a bench reading near the Fontaine de Médicis. 'Would you care to converse?' he had asked with such real tentativeness and gentleness that I closed my book. New life would not be found in a Penguin Classic, not that fall afternoon. We spoke a little, then kissed, lightly first, then deeply; this was our conversation on the shaded bench near the fountain. The discovery of our shared urgency, the boy's and mine, had perhaps caused the climb to his room to seem longer than it was, since now when I return to this quarter to look for the building, the houses are all similarly tall, which is to say only slightly, and I no longer recognize my own past. It had been a convent, he said, by which he meant monastery, and the street was extremely old, as old as the Roman city Lutèce. Maybe the idea of a monastery had enlarged the building in my recollection, or maybe it was simply the thought of its ancientness that had performed the transformation. When Jeanne Duval lived in this neighbourhood, in the late 1830s, it was home to several popular theatres frequented by students, and it was already ancient. This is where Abelard had lived and conducted his famous sad studies with Heloise, and it had been the site of the university ever since. My idealism was capacious; I was not immune to such mythologies. They accented the suffused desire that seemed to spread from my afternoon encounter over the architecture and the streets.

Jeanne Duval's second-floor apartment, fashionably and unsparingly decorated with Persian chintz, had been near by on the rue Saint-Georges, said Félix Nadar in his little book on Baudelaire, close to the Pantheon Theatre, where she often played at that time. This theatre was installed in a long-desanctified church, Church of the Cordeliers, where, during the Revolution, a Jacobin club had met. The church is now gone, but Nadar describes the unique charm of the theatrical installation, the way the stage and backdrop and wings were set up in the boarded-up choir, the curtain attached to the carved overhead mouldings, with the spectators seated in the nave. He describes Jeanne's tallness and her slender waist and the beautiful coppery colour of her skin, her magnificent hair, her deep voice, her reserve, her remarkable carriage, and given this stature and elegance, her incongruous role of housemaid, the first time he saw her play.

Duval was just one of the names Jeanne went by; her birth name was perhaps her mother's, Lemaire. Much later she changed the spelling to Lemer. Perhaps her stage name was Berthe. Nadar may have photographed her under this name. Or the photograph of the actress taken by Nadar was not Jeanne Duval, but another younger women, also of mixed family background, but otherwise not similar. For a time she was named Prosper. Perhaps she was evading creditors; perhaps it was a way of inventing herself continuously; maybe she just didn't care for the fixity of names. In her way she was a philosopher, said Baudelaire. She was born around 1820, it is agreed, or perhaps it was later, on an island, perhaps Haiti, perhaps Réunion, of African and French parentage, and came to France as young as fifteen. Nadar said she was very tall. Her walk was famous. Baudelaire compared her to a ship at sail. She powdered her face to lighten it, but not her hands, said Nadar. Was she fifteen when she met Baudelaire? Some say so. Perhaps she was one quarter black, it was said, with all the obscenity of such a measuring. Her identification papers were lost in a fire. Perhaps her mother accompanied her; perhaps Mme.

Lemaire had been born in Nantes in a brothel and died in Paris in 1852. Perhaps her mother's funeral expenses were provided by Baudelaire. Perhaps Jeanne had a stroke in Honfleur in 1859 when she was living there with Baudelaire; perhaps Baudelaire found a hospice for her recovery in Paris, near the Porte Saint-Denis. Perhaps she remained paralyzed on one side. By the time Manet painted her in 1862, reclining with a fan and almost overpowered by the glorious white crinolined dress, her finely shod feet and slender ankles emerging in the foreground from beneath the belling skirt, her face very small and far-off as a result of the foreshortened perspective, perhaps she was suffering, or her vision was failing, or she was consumptive. Her hollow eyes are very dark. Perhaps she had syphilis; so perhaps did Baudelaire. Perhaps he continued to rent her an apartment, cover her expenses, and pay for her housemaid until the time of his own stroke in 1866. He kept Manet's portrait of his mistress in the clinic until he died, said his friends. It is certain that all her letters to him were burned by his mother, who refused his sincere request to provide for Jeanne after his death. His family had hated Jeanne Duval because she wasn't white and because she was an actress. Perhaps she was seen by Nadar on the boulevards, hobbling with crutches, as late at 1869. Baudelaire called her Mistress of Mistresses, She-Beast, Black Venus, Giantess, Féline, Angel, Vampire, Wife, Witch, Philosopher, Nymph. They were together, loving and fighting and talking, for twenty-one years.

Théodore de Banville said that Jeanne Duval was the only woman Baudelaire ever loved, 'this Jeanne who he always and so magnificently sung.' Banville and Jeanne had met at the home of friends before he made Baudelaire's acquaintance, she dressed in a ravishing velvet cap, her heavy dark blue wool dress trimmed with gold piping. She spoke to Banville of *Monsieur Baudelaire* – always she was to call her lover *Monsieur*, ironically, I would think – and his beautiful furniture, his collections, his obsessions. He buffed his fingernails and composed a sonnet, she said to Banville, with the same fastidiousness. They were all then about twenty years old. Banville says, as a strange proof of the poet's love, that Baudelaire would place Jeanne in a low armchair before him in the sunlight, simply to passively adore her at length, occasionally reading her some verse, although she did not much like his poems.

There transpired in the glossy yellow room a heaviness, not violence but an immaterial forcefulness, a sort of spiritual smothering – smothering was the analogy I used in my diary for the metaphysical sensation – which I felt embarrassed to perceive as pleasure, even though there was a scrim of physical satisfaction in the act. Ambivalently I perceived my attraction to my own weakness. The sliding from desire to the heaviness was swift, and had its own power of enticement, an inarguable velocity. Briefly the feeling of being possessed was my inner decoration. The boy said that women were meant to be loved and perfumed and dressed, and I, so shabbily groomed, so conscious of my partial dispossession of the female ideal, did not wish to immediately disagree, although I did not concur with the sentiment. It was maybe an Old World thing to say. He said that he liked my Nordic skin; *Nordic* was what he called my type. And he whispered to me phrases about the regard and the heartbeat. He seemed to speak in song lyrics, pop songs I myself then sang along to.

I thought that I would not go back and then I did. I went to the glossy yellow room for the thoroughness of the representation we enacted, the strangely freeing totality of being submerged in the banal representation, in the song of possession, because I was curious. It was a form of theatre; I was both an actor and the witness. And as an actor, I was, for myself, both an attending figure of service – a sort of handmaid – and the lead. In this second self-dramatization I was mistaken, but that didn't prevent the erotic thrill of the delusion. Maybe I was studying the present in the way that I knew how, like someone not quite of the present. It seemed easy, until it wasn't. I would visit rooms like this yellow one. Others strolled on boulevards. Not all of the present was accessible. Some threads would always be bunched up, tangled, hidden on the reverse side of the garment. There, unseen, they would chafe the wearer.

Originally Courbet had depicted Jeanne Duval standing behind the poet in *The Artist's Studio*. Her head is tilted downward to the right, as if she's reading over Baudelaire's shoulder. She seems to be holding a fan, but maybe it's a mirror, and as he reads, she maybe looks down at her own reflection. The image is quite difficult to make out; she's been painted over by the artist. This erasure, most of the critical texts agree, but without citing any source for the assumption, was at Baudelaire's request. Many years later, as if in a mystic, material refusal of this obliteration, her figure became visible again; through a chemical process of degradation, the paint lost some of its initial opacity. Now, if one cares to search, or especially if studying photographs of the painting, it is just possible to make out Jeanne's present but absent form behind the poet, the oblique slant of her neck, the top of her voluminous skirt belling out from her slight waist. Some say that the couple had been fighting, and temporarily split, which was the reason Jeanne was removed from the image. I don't know. I can surmise that Baudelaire's own banal shame over the colour of his mistress's skin spurred the decision, that and his desire to hide their relationship from the scornful gaze of his family. The poet was not as socially expansive as his own construction of erotic beauty.

Baudelaire claimed that beauty always contained something bizarre; *bizarre* had been his exact word, which is to say: difficult to understand, because of its strangeness. Singular. When I pause with Baudelaire's word, when I halt the automatic transposition from his French to my English, my feeling for his thinking deepens. The French word is related to *bigarré* – diversely coloured. In the baroque French of the Low Countries it was a word used for extremely valuable striated tulips. Yet the Italian form, used by Dante, meant angry – specifically the quality of quick flashes of anger. Then it entered courtesans' language in the sixteenth century. *Bizarre* carries within it noisy outbursts, livid flushes, concubinage, and extravagant mixture. In old Spanish and Portuguese it meant brave, handsome. Did he think of Jeanne in these ways? It seems clear that Jeanne Duval was bizarre to Baudelaire in every sense of the word's movements and histories. He exoticized her hair, and skin, and scent so intensely that *Les Fleurs du mal* seems to be composed of her hair, and skin, and scent. Also her gait, and her origins, or a myth of her origins, in a picturesque framing of the mixture and distance she was constrained to express. It's not difficult for me to imagine that Baudelaire, with a grossly inevitable racism, was incapable of acknowledging to the bourgeois art-viewing public of Paris, by means of his portrait together with Jeanne, his relationship to the beauty he enjoyed privately in her second-floor room on the Montagne Sainte-Geneviève, and later at many other addresses. Such an erasure could then pass as tact. It is a very ugly possibility for the poet of beauty. But there are alternate theories. Some say that it was Courbet's promoter, the critic Champfleury, who demanded Jeanne's erasure from the painting. He is depicted seated in a black suit, between Baudelaire and Courbet. Champfleury was the critical champion of the new realism; a friend also of Baudelaire's since the forties, he had become a novelist of renown. In his own 1857 text *Le réalisme*, he rejected poetry in terms that mirror a typified horror of female sexuality: 'a proliferating substance, in submission to fashion, and in some way inexhaustible.' I want to believe it was Champfleury, not Baudelaire, who chose to erase the image of Jeanne Duval. This painting was made in 1848, the year of the height of Baudelaire's friendship with Courbet, and it was not exhibited until 1855. Jeanne's erasure took place during the preparation for exhibition, several years after the painting was nominally completed, just after it had been rejected by the Exposition Universelle. In the years between, there had been a shift in the friendship of the two men, particularly in Baudelaire's assessment of Courbet. Both were supporters and briefly participants in the 1848 February Revolution, when King Louis Philippe was ousted for an elected Republican government. Their friendship formed at this time. Courbet was an impassioned working-class provincial; Baudelaire was an angry, dispossessed bourgeois son who at that time identified with and shared many of the struggles of outsiders and the poor. Near the end of his life, thinking back to this period, he wrote: 'My intoxication in 1848 … Desire of vengeance. Natural pleasure in demolishing. 1848 was amusing only because everyone was building Utopias like castles in Spain. 1848 was charming only by the very excess of the ridiculous.' It's a retroactive scorn; in his youth he did actively desire the dissolution of the old hierarchies, preserved in the bogus monarchy. He hated his stepfather, who for him represented everything about the old power that the revolutionaries wanted to erase. So in the collective intoxication of the 1840s, the poet and the painter agreed on an enemy: the king, along with the class that gained their prestige from him. But within three years the Revolution failed, and that public failure acted as a lens on their private differences. By 1851, Louis-Napoleon, the elected president of the Second Republic, had staged a coup d'état, and in 1852, he named himself Emperor Napoleon III: the country reverted to the monarchy that would last until 1870. Not only had the Revolution failed, the new regime was explicitly an empire of capital. Courbet quickly assumed the rhetoric of the new city of money, while Baudelaire completely and scornfully withdrew from the possibility of politics to his bare hotels.

In those hotels, which are public and private, and so studio-like, as well as spiritual and intellectual and sexual in marbled-through cosmographic mixture, everything does happen. Somebody weeps, somebody fucks, somebody writes a poem, somebody leaves their panties to dry on the window latch. Somebody sleeps late and dreams a novel and somebody who is late tries on all their clothes in serial frustration. Something leaks and there is mouse shit in the drawer. Strangers pretend they can love one another, which is sometimes the case. A spill of strange perfume on a red carpet has altered the mood of an era. Or humiliation finds its architecture.

In one of those rooms, I once exploded in anger at some rote insult. He threw down my book; I slapped his face. Next I felt the banal boy's full weight behind thumbs crushing down on my trachea, his weight on my chest. This is a sure way to halt speech. With the flint-hard thought that I was experiencing my death, and a spark of surprise at the terminal simplicity of the fact, consciousness stopped. Now new time erupts – my dull shock at the fact of my aliveness – the boy having meanwhile vacated the little scene of my body. With my painful collar of bruises, the whites of my eyes engorged with blood (I wanted to say *slobbering rubies* to dignify the injury, I wanted to *be* the words of Mallarmé writing his tomb for Baudelaire, but I myself was the tomb, I was the tomb of what, I wasn't sure, the tomb of literature – immortal pubis – or at very least the ruin), I ejected myself into the Paris night and I walked, carrying with me always now that inner piece of ruby, of flint, the tomb of what poem. The girl.

In Baudelaire's Paris, Napoleon III had seized control of publication, banking, and city space. This was the domestic expression of his expanding colonizing activities, in Algeria, in Indo-China, in New Caledonia, in Senegal; during his reign, France's overseas territory tripled. In that Paris he hired Haussmann to impose a city-wide system of boulevards by razing the worker neighbourhoods, appropriating thousands of degraded residential buildings, then selling the sites to developers. Entire neighbourhoods disappeared, and their inhabitants were displaced. Strictly policed censorship laws were a linguistic takeover of the city streets by the bankers. The restriction of daily lives paralleled capital's more historically legible colonizations. The old street trades were monitored and controlled – street-singers, often provincial or foreign, until then unruly participants in a radically populist movement of news and politics in the city, were newly required to submit all of their songs to censors. Through the revolutionary period their song lyrics, set to popular tunes, had been renegade modes of publication. Song then was public and helped to form new publics. These previously itinerant artists were, in Haussmann's new Paris, issued licences, in the form of brass tags that they were required to visibly wear. These were renewable every three months, needing repeated registration with the police. Singers could no longer wander, they were forbidden to sell their lyrics as pamphlets, and they were permitted to perform only the officially approved songs in a few designated squares. The censorship exerted on literary publishing was thorough also; in 1857, Baudelaire's *Les Fleurs du mal* and Flaubert's *Madame Bovary* were tried under the new anti-obscenity laws for damaging public morals.

Public morals are so vulnerable. A poem or a novel will endanger them, a young girl's desire will offend them, the skin colour of one's lover will diminish them. I long for moral abundance, an obscene flourishing of the category of morality. We can admit more, rather than less, embellish the capaciousness of the idea of the public. If I was a monstrous slut, if I close to disappeared, if I confused aesthetics with the feeling of bodily risk, if I mistook ideology for sensation, anger for bravery, if I belatedly evaded an ambivalent erasure, I was in very good company.

Only the poet was found guilty, and it is pertinent to say that of the two writers, Baudelaire lived more thoroughly and wilfully outside the systems of influence and power. Politics had become one arm of money. There was little that he hated more than money, and little that he needed as much. Courbet all the while revelled in the new publicity culture, adapting his art to promotional schemes, like his Pavilion of Realism. For Baudelaire, worse than Courbet's success was the fact that it was based on an appropriation of the poet's early concept of beauty – that beauty must be modern, it must be of the current moment. Courbet deformed the urgency of modern beauty to arrive at his aesthetic of realism; the real for the painter was a materialist representation only. For Baudelaire, the realism of beauty was also and necessarily immaterial, immersed in spiritual and subjective circulations. One part of beauty, irreal, would defy and resist the censors and the bankers. This was beauty's political imaginary. It was not for appearance only. Beauty must be angry. *If* Baudelaire had instructed Courbet to erase the image of Jeanne Duval from the allegorical canvas, Courbet's shameless embrace of monetized display was part of the demand. Courbet appropriated beauty to money. His allegory was the market.

Baudelaire, so bitterly wracked with ambivalence, with rejection and debt, anachronistically repudiated the ideology of capital. His realism would recognize the spiritual complexity of dispossessed lives. He undoubtedly projected his aesthetic emotions on those outsiders cursed by Haussmann's city; he loved actresses, street singers, old women, acrobats, and prostitutes. He loved Jeanne Duval. He reconstructed the baroque city he required in *Le Spleen de Paris*, a city whose equivocity could enfold both pleasure and doubt. In Baudelaire's cosmos, bizarre beauty was necessarily striated with irony, anger, and refusal.

The old pleasure had been lost, and the new had not yet been made. Jeanne's body was not her body; it was the field of an aesthetic proclamation and its withdrawal. Her body was the ground for the refracted self-identity of these bohemian cadets. Carmine-bronze-violet-tinted-blue-black, they described her to one another; they recognized each other by means of the screen of her skin. She lived, as I said, on the second floor, facing the court, with her blonde maid Louise. They had no cook and no kitchen, so the two women would go to eat together in restaurants. Their home was open to any who wished to pay a visit, and from these guests she asked for nothing, since the household was entirely provided for by her lover, Baudelaire. Furthermore she was free, said Nadar, to accept any intimate attentions, since at that time their youthful circle regarded monogamy as a sort of crime. In the afternoon, between the hours of two and four only, her door was closed; this was when Monsieur would visit her, and also every night.

Banville had first met Baudelaire strolling in the Luxembourg Gardens, by means of their common friend, the journalist Privat d'Anglemont. '*Tiens,*' Privat d'Anglemont said to his companion, at the sight of the approach of the young poet through the foliage, '*c'est Baudelaire*': Baudelaire, with his little pointy beard, nipped-in black velvet smock, and silver-headed walking stick, who seemed to have stepped from a van Dyck. And then the three men spent the entire night walking together in the city.

In the morning we had more whisky, and chocolate. I was puffy and slick and my lips were kissed raw, and I went to vomit behind the plastic curtain. Magnificent. There was no need for modesty. This is what beauty was for in some songs. Some say they only flirted, but my song was not that one. Later he asked if I would care to be prostituted. No, I said.

If he could pimp, I could write.

TWILIGHT

Further to the stupidity of poetry, here I will tell about the most beautiful poem I ever wrote: I once bled out a stain on a restaurant chair, which revealed to my backwards glance a map of the arrondissements of Paris – a crooked reddish-pink spiral bisected by the serpentine slash that was the Seine. This stain was the augury that brought me to my borrowed city.

What I wanted of this city, this stain, was a site for the kind of freedom I sought. Supernatural, sexual, artificial, blooming on one side.

Part loss, part object, the stain, with its irregular, permeable border, its ingressions and turbulences, its fragmentary, metonymic nature, its abundance of nested contours, limitless saturation, elisions of propriety, its regime of discontinuity and contamination, was an operating force at once fractal, mystic, and obscene. My analysis of its irregularities is shameless, followed nonetheless by a small retroactive flicker of shame, which is mildly stimulating. Like a convex mirror or a cosmology, the stain revealed a macrocosm: it was a dream city, a city within a city, a mirror within a tableau. It brought me to painting and it brought me to verse. It brought me to the impure repetition of the Baudelairean authorship within myself, its formerness and presentness entangling or continuously supplementing one another without cancelling the tenuous autonomy of the authorship itself, which seemed now to wander, seeking perhaps a temporary room within which to surge into new time, stainlike, much as Baudelaire had wandered in claustrophobic decors, in unconscious imitation of his master Poe. Within Poe's texts the younger poet had fallen into the shadow of his own future thinking, already latent, with the haunted sense that he himself had already authored what he read. The stain retroactively transmits a singularity that evades the personal. Everything will be the same without being identical. I'll be a feminine man whose decadent joy resists all appropriation. I'll be untimely only.

Now we live some distance from the time of stains. We live some distance from freedom. Vigorously and joyfully, sometimes glassily, extremely anachronistically – for who would ever now with any sincerity speak of truth – at other times with a fragile paper-like feeling, I may put this beautiful truth-speaking in whose mouth? I shall put it in my own female mouth. Here I assume the stain, the stained character that transmits. I'm Hazel Brown, newly Baudelairean, the repetition of a stain animated with consciousness, pigment awash in ectoplasm. Desire awash.

The Spanish philosophy student on the marble inner stairs of the nighttime apartment building; the way he removed his glasses first to clean them with the corner of his white cotton shirt. He had approached me in a café to admire my little sketches. The sideways curve of his charming member. His charming affection for Dionysus. On those marble steps I grew the sultry wings of an angel.

The young American banker who had come to Paris to buy suits, in his dull posh hotel that I left immediately after.

He could not kiss. The dark suits there out in the room in their garment bags like witnesses to an unclimactic ineptitude.

The Argentinian Hegelian who worked as a hotel clerk on the boulevard Saint-Michel, in the utopian minimalism of the student room at the Cité Universitaire. His shy lisp. Drinking linden flower tea in the night. The whispered entanglement of our two accents.

(These recollections today, Reader – the curve, the marble, the whispered dialectic – as a hard June rain splits open the unripe cherries on the tree, rots the linden flowers before they can be picked for tisane. I did then like the beauty of the boys. I'd be their glamorous thing and then I wouldn't.)

Like most girls I knew then, trapped folklorically in their fantasy of beauty, I believed that beauty would be a part of freedom. For some time, in various settings and registers, like a scientist of freedom, I earnestly tested this belief, the belief in the necessary relationship between beauty and freedom. I really did strive. I imagined this as a pagan research. My intentions were as ardent as they were inauthentic. I had stepped into a quite common mistake. Really it was more of a pit than a mistake, but at least I would not be alone there. For my beloveds, I strove to represent beauty, without first understanding the structure of the idea of beauty. Some's desire was a money and it bought them largesse; others' desire made them poorer. Still others were the unwilling currency. In my unwittingly conservative gestures towards beauty, I was miming an ancient literary protocol, not having yet reached my current conclusion, which is that literature is the worst theology.

For the bookish girl, any conventional identification could only be disastrous. Sometimes the identification was inadvertent. What seemed like aesthetic sentiment would be belatedly revealed as the promotion of a spiritual straitening. Within this constraint, always the conjuring of the representation of beauty felt effortful and false. It was a form of service work. Never would I execute the beautiful tasks with the required charitable attitude. Never would I be paid squarely. The currency was all wrong, as well as the amount. Everything mortal about me was off. My sunburn, my swollen appetites, my hunger, my frown lines. Repeatedly the striving to synchronize my desires with the representation brought me no pleasure. Eventually the mortal stain would show. Doggedly I tried to get it right. There would be outbursts and scenes. I came to see that in the literary theology, beauty was associated with immobility, which is to say, my immobility, the conceptual immobility of the girl or thing. Whether with tenderness or with force, beauty was to be acted upon, purchased, sat in its chair in the light. Beauty would incite the purchaser's beautiful speech. Oh, I could not be that thing for long, although often I did admire it in the literature. I did fail the literary beauty in this way. I did reveal my stain, the ever-movable indelible stain. For wasn't this girldom I had been assigned a long covert transmission or inheritance of a stain? At first the theft of beauty by the market of the literati didn't bother me; I was trained into the contract by my habitual reading. But then it did bother me; it saddened me considerably. I felt the sadness thoroughly. I believed it then. I wrote the sadness in my diary, I drank the sadness in my room or in cafés, I fucked the sadness. I almost believed I was the sadness. But I could not go all the way. Sadness did not utterly disappear; transformations aren't clean. Finally I preferred to have been interpolated by a stain. I discovered that it was not a loss: the stain was a thinking. Because I preferred to survive, I entered the aesthetics of doubt. With the interruption of my identification with beauty by the stain, a philosophy arrived. It was a little tool towards freedom.

My youthful commitment to the identity of beauty with freedom had been experimental, in the sense that usefully recognizing oneself as a girl was an experiment. I had absorbed the commitment from the literature, trying it on like a rhetoric that I called passion, loving the interior thrill of difference I felt as the tiny identifications operated within me, interpreting the thrill as my own emotion, not recognizing that what this thrill covered over was a worried questioning, not yet linguistic, about the scorn that bordered beauty's literary description. The man-poets scorned what they desired; their sadistic money was such that the object scorned was endowed with the shimmer of sex. How radiant we were in our gorgeous outfits and our bad moods! Oh, and this ignited poetry. Baudelaire scorned Jeanne Duval and every female he dallied with, or at least did so on paper, Ted Hughes scorned Sylvia Plath, Ezra Pound scorned Djuna Barnes, George Baker scorned Elizabeth Smart, everybody scorned Jean Rhys. Proust did not scorn Albertine because Albertine was a man. The she-poets perished beneath the burden of beauty and scorn. This is what I observed. This was the formal sexuality of lyric. Who was I then, what was I, when I, a girl, was their reader, the reader of the beautiful representations? Who was I if I became the describer, and how could I become this thing before perishing? Would I then even recognize myself? Because I saw the perishing everywhere. Daily I read it. The freedom of desiring and its potent transformations seemed not to belong to beauty, just to beauty's describer. Anyone without a language for desire perishes. Any girl-thing. My questions emerged then as a mute, troubled resistance to the ancient operation that I also craved. Certainly the poem must become something other than this contract. I seemed to have been wrong about most things, except for my will to write and to read. That and the stain. Even so, I did not want to give up on beauty altogether, so gently I set it to the side, and with it the philosophical potency and freedom of the bad mood. Certainly I would return to beauty, I would return to the bad mood. I would arrive at anger.

For now I would continue to test the hypothesis of lust. I would test it in bookshops, in museums, and at fountains. I would test it, as I have described, in attic rooms, maid's rooms as they were called. As unfixed lust, in fact a maid, I would write, I would perambulate and peruse. I would forget not to stare. I would move towards what I desired. I would make myself understood. What I wrote about in my heavy hard-bound diary: about a girl living in a room, getting dressed, buying food, fucking, the goddamned tulips ugly in the dark. These were historical records about things that might never have before existed, if I were to judge by the literature. Before I began to write what I needed to write, an event that, to my considerable dissatisfaction, would not begin for some years (lines such as 'even the musking tulips' would assert themselves, unwelcome even at the moment of transcription), I had to set the record straight, establish an archive. This would be my foundation. I had to describe everything, from the perspective of the lust of a maid. I did it altruistically, for the future. It would not be attractive. It would show my unkindness, the banality of my appetites, the small lies I told, the wilful omissions. My descriptions would not be about being seen, nor about the striving for that position within the lyric contract. Being seen by money was a form of incarceration within an enforced aesthetic constraint. Within this contract, aesthetic judgments are the same judgments that assess financial risk. Is the girl productive? Lucrative? Accessible? Against this odious assessment, I began the slow accumulation of the documents of the incommensurable procedures, procedures for which I was not a sign, but an untrained actor, a bad actor, a hack of a sentence writer, an anonymous fuck. If the result seems merely decorative, ornamental, it's because now realism has become another name for capital.

If I repeat the word *girl* very often, it's for those who, like me, prefer the short monosyllable, its percussive force. I wonder if in repeating I might exhaust the designation that fixed me, flood it with the lugubrious excess it named, and so convert the diminutive syllable to a terrain of the possible. Maybe this would be grace. Maybe. Would it be grace to aesthetically yield to the mystic obscenity of the word *girl*? She is allegorical, her body both lost and grotesquely multiple. She is estranged in a ruinous nostalgia for decorative immobility, enclosure, muteness. I want to force the category to produce, monstrously, a subjectivity outside subjection.

The diaries are grubby and worn and release little scraps as I handle them– paper tea-bag wrappings, a pencilled note from Minou on a scrap of torn envelope, receipts and calculations, an unpaid doctor's bill handwritten in blue ink, amateurish cross-hatched drawings of Michelangelo's slaves. I've brought them across three decades in my motley suitcases, cushioned by woollen coats. I've dragged them across odd thresholds, storing them at the back of musty armoires, bringing them out again, moving on. Now that they have become entirely impersonal, stained relics of a departed political economy, I, at the age of fifty-five, shall make of these diaries, here in this penurious retreat, a portrait of my luck.

The aging dandiacal gigolo in the cream-coloured linen suit whom, after a long evening of Latin Quarter jazz bars, I rejected, by the Fontaine Saint-Michel battling Lucifer. He called himself an architect. Lucifer's Miltonic handsomeness. Oh, the going-with and the departing, my pantheistic intoxication with the leaflike erotics of number: I wanted the men to yield the obscenity I craved, I wanted the frieze of their bodies to decorate the complete alterity of my ambition. The making of this frieze opened the technology of a gentle heresy. How else could I recognize disorder? Any loving girl could only be heretical. I recognize her heresy here.

My portrait photograph of Minou in her black bowler hat, sometime companion who in her Southern drawl introduced me to Djuna Barnes, who kept beguilingly anarchic scrapbooks in her tiny top-storey room in the Beat hotel on rue Gît-le-Coeur, who wandered the Marais in search of angels, whether of stone or flesh: she is on a bench with the bell tower of Saint-Sulpice behind, Lucifer dancing on her hat brim. The constellation of fine moles on her elegant profile.

I did not, at that time, enter Saint-Sulpice, the baroque church where Baudelaire had been baptized, to visit the chapel with the Delacroix paintings of the storming of the temple, and Jacob battling the angel, and here too the struggle of Michael and Lucifer, all swirling with chatoyant pastels; I did not then even know of the paintings, described in 1861 by Baudelaire as badly situated, the high chapel window disgorging an oblique, destructive light, though at the time of the black diary with the pebbled black board covers, I lived very close by, on the rue du Cherche-Midi. I had sublet a seventh-storey maid's room from an Irish actress for a month. It was called a room; it had a window, and also a telephone, very luxurious commodity. But it was little more than the width of the mattress, which I would roll up in the day to sit and write near the window at the foot of the narrow space. The actress's furnishings included this pallet and its coverings, a low wooden stool on which the telephone sat, near the door a blue dresser on which I kept my minimal kitchen accoutrements – coffee pot, cutting board, bowl, pocket knife – an alcove filled with homemade, bowing shelves, where she had stacked quantities of her colourful clothing, and to the right of the window a small, pink, marble-topped, wax-splattered vanity table upon which leaned a mirror, and a battered and tarnished saxophone draped with a mauve feather boa. I placed my typewriter on this table, and it was here that I would write, sometimes covering the mirror with a paisley silk scarf, sometimes examining my face with an incredulous curiosity, believing that in the oblique light already I could see the marks of age. Undoubt-edly, she applied her makeup here. There was a communal, rust-marked sink with cold-water faucet at the end of the corridor, beside the shared toilet. I bought a plastic basin to fill at that sink and bring back to my room, and I washed in cold water that afterwards I poured out into the mansard roof gutters beneath my window. Out on the windowsill I stored my food. I had everything I needed, in a slightly diminished, awkward scale, as if I lived my life reduced by one sixth of the dimensions usually considered necessary. This awkward contraction of domestic necessity was for me utopian. The minor discomfort, unimportant in itself, was a subtle threshold to a different sensing. I poured my nightpiss also into that gutter.

These upper-storey rooms belonged to the bourgeois inhabitants of the lower floors, and unlike the curved marble steps and wrought-iron railings leading to those apartments, the upper rooms were accessed by a different, narrow back stairway. Georges Perec, in *Life: A User's Manual*, his byzantine biography of a Paris apartment house, begins his story by describing the building's stairway, which he characterizes as a neutral space, belonging to all and to none. 'All that passes,' he says, 'passes by the stairs, and all that comes, comes by the stairs.' But each apartment house has two sets of stairs, and they are not equal. All do not pass by the same stairs. There are the ritually ornate stairs of the bourgeoisie, decked with curlicues that dignify their ascent or demise, and there are the more dour, neutral stairs of service. Ours were the service stairs. This humbler approach was overseen scrupulously by the concierge in her glassed-in observation post. For maids need surveillance. Without the constant gaze of the concierge to monitor her guests, any maid could at any moment make the turn to prostitution. Since a maid is essentially a slut, as far as the bourgeoisie is concerned. As for the artists who occupied the upper rooms, like maids and sluts they too served the middle classes. They would never cease to be dependent on middle-class need, Perec says, so they also required surveillance.

Poetry, too, I would later learn, has its concierges. Poetry, too, I would enter by the dowdy back stair. When I had seemingly left my life of service, and had found what at first seemed like grander, or at least more autonomous, rooms to frequent, I would learn that I was well prepared for literature. Having fled domestic labour, I began my literary service with commercial freelance work, as an art critic and book reviewer, rather than by observing the then-normative academic protocols. I had already attended the academy of sentence writing, within my diaries; this training was thorough enough. Of the two modes of entry, it is very likely that the back stair is the more pleasurable, and the company more varied. I had experience with the service stair.

Our attic rooms had once lodged the domestic servants employed by each bourgeois household to care for their children, cook their meals, clean their flats, but now these bare chambers were cheaply let out by the apartment owners to those of us who tried to live outside money. Many of us were what you could call foreign, or women, or writers. Some of us were not legal. There being then no bylaws or rules regarding the supply of plumbing, heating, or the other hygienic improvements of the twentieth century within casually rented quarters, I suppose it had become slightly more profitable to rent the spartan rooms for cash to girls in fugue than to lodge the help there. It was to me a strangely inverted living arrangement: we moneyless ones floated above the wealth, with access to the sky, entertained by their upwards-drifting piano scales and cello practice, their domestic spats about money, whereas in the New World cities I knew, we occupied damp basements, as the ancestors would, or pagan gods. Up there in our maid's rooms we coolly and disinterestedly skimmed and carried on, above the fiscal dramas of the bourgeois strivings. Time above was baroque, contrapuntal; we relived a dream of the time of some other long century, unsure if it was the time of the future, or of the past. It wove through the present, where it was cited, in fragments, but retained an aesthetic autonomy. We called this poetry. Maybe it was a kind of heaven. We found these anachronistic rooms by word of mouth, in bookshops or on church bulletin boards, and fibbed a little to the owners in order to procure their heavy skeleton keys: phantom jobs or pretended stipends supplemented our unspeakable economies. Also, we shared – Dutch Peter, the skinny, stooped, floppy-haired novelist who lived down the corridor, would let me heat my coffee pot on his little camping burner sometimes, and as I waited for the pot to boil, he would, from his desk at the window, tell me in his soft voice about the difficulty of writing. Thank you, Peter. He seemed to me to be a person entirely outside of age. He could have been twenty-seven or he could have been fifty. He had recently seen a man shot dead on the street, on a busy afternoon on the rue de Rivoli. Was it political or personal? We would never know. The newspapers never mentioned it. He was haunted by this brutal assassination, and soon afterward went back to Amsterdam.

Each of us would innovate little methods for survival. I would take to my narrow bed in the cold room and write lists as if they could scaffold me. Room, 350 francs; coffee pot, 50 francs; electric burner, 150 francs (for I had to buy one after Dutch Peter left); face cloths, 28 francs; a little coffee at a café, 5 francs; and that bloody whisky that was 23 francs. Read Boethius, Olson, Proust, Rhys, Berger, Nabokov, Durrell, Plath. I wonder now who reads Durrell with the breathlessness he then commanded? Read Rilke, Barthes, and Dante. Read Heidegger. Read Woolf and Levertov. I navigated amongst books by an uneven mixture of gut and chance, and so my choices were mostly conventional. I mention them here as a portrait of a style of readerly ardour in 1985. Being itinerant, I had no access yet to libraries. It was the year before I read Arendt and Mallarmé. I had stumbled curiously within Wittgenstein without becoming committed, experiencing his thought as a style of retreat, and I had hovered over the surface of *Our Lady of the Flowers* in a stunned pre-masturbatory glaze. In Proust I lingered on the dress descriptions, with a flame of astonishment. Who was Fortuny? In reading I continuously discovered the extent my own incomprehension; it was so varied and complicated that it became my wealth.

Reading, listing, I wanted to escape the violent sociology of beauty to experience aesthetics as an even redistribution of the senses across the most banal parts of dailiness. I wanted to write it all down, everything inchoate: light, dust, textile, pigment, sentences. Beauty would be the lust for the complex, unspoken surface of the present. I sought a sense-textile, which would flourish outside the humiliating economy of servitude that names us. Within any day there is a hidden dimension both occult and common. The senses might operate on several temporal levels simultaneously, remaining partly in the hidden dimension, as they also eased outwards in the way that, for example, if one had made love all afternoon in the room, one later carried a different thinking into the evening streets and also into books. Perception opened, and surface became epistemology. Each category of experience continuously transformed into another. Describing was a way of trying to understand anything about freedom. I believed that there would always be kinds of time that escaped sociology. I made an invisible art of describing, to get to the core of how it works. When I say 'art,' I mean the quotidian commitment to a set of techniques, some received, some by necessity invented. I wanted this art to be unrecognizable, to keep it for my own pleasure, and so I read and I walked; I became part of images. Images did exist, but differently than I had first believed, and I couldn't contain them or quantify them. They were borderless and moved between sensations. John Berger, in an essay on Caravaggio, once spoke of the universe on the other side of the skin, a phrase that lodged itself in my imaginary for years. Were there kinds of images that were not part of the dire contract of beauty and scorn? How did one comprehend this other universe? I pondered in my diary whether one could ever become an image for oneself, an image to live from, or at least to write from, confounding something Charles Olson had said in one of the excitingly opaque essays in a pale grey paperback from New Directions. This image would not be a means of appearing to a social given; rather, it would be the self-given permission to not disappear to oneself. When I recognize afresh the courage it takes for any girl to not disappear to herself, I am still shocked. Could the image of my own self-appearance open a possible world? This query sometimes felt false, because in my experience then it was without category, so worked on the plane of intuition, but I trained myself to embrace its falsity. I wanted the image to be kinetic and tactile, an undulant elsewhere, not the predetermined fixture of a gaze, not the token of a bordered exchange. I wanted it to be rhythmic, in the way that Benveniste spoke about rhythm: not a measure, not a temporal phenomena of Nature, but 'the form in the instant that it is assumed by what is moving, mobile and fluid, the form of what does not have organic consistency.' A girl has no organic consistency. In this invented discipline of images, I gradually lost all fear of distortion. I perhaps oozed, rather than thought. What united and separated things? An imperceptible membrane, stretchy, spangled, gauzelike, of total vitality, which included laziness. A crystalline gel. An alphabet. Laziness in fact was my main form of vitality. It was my portal to the truth of artifice. Artifice was to become my calling.

The season was now mid-winter. Preoccupied as I was with painting, when I crossed the river during my dissolute walks, I didn't pass by the Louvre without entering. By preference I went late in the day. Unlike the chilly maid's room, it was warm in the museum, and I relished the quietness of the galleries – for a scant few, just those of the currently agreed-upon masterpieces, were typically frequented. The wide upholstered benches, the subtle camaraderie of the uniformed attendants, the mysterious, enticing glimpses afforded by the elegant enfilade of room into room, the dull glow of the heavy gilt frames, the thrum of building systems, the lesser rhythm of the underdetermined and precise descriptive labels that I loved to list in my notebook: all this initiated me into a drifting euphoria. It was rather like the solipsistic pleasure of very slowly skimming a book in late afternoon without truly reading, enjoying the pleasure of turning the pages and moving the eyes across print, revelling in its mute materiality without bothering about the intricacies of meaning. I could read Latin this way; for a long time it was the way I read French. Painting, too, was an opaque language. Here the idea of elsewhere achieved a charged materiality. What some people experienced in crowds, amongst strange faces, on boulevards or in department stores – and this is what Poe had written of, the

calm yet inquisitive interest in everything, without differen-
tiation – seized me in these long galleries of paintings. Many
I glimpsed only in passing, if I were searching out a single
gallery or era and became a little lost in the sprawling wings
of the long building. But even the inattentive, hurried passage
could present an unsought but essential encounter, in the
way that a single, unknown face can urgently address one
with its depths of attractive strangeness, when passing in a
crowd. This elsewhere of faces, of paintings, of pages, seems
to break open time, which is the punctum I searched for
among the surfaces. I mean there's an unbeckoned flash of
limitlessness that can open for an instant within the propriety
of the human face, or the painted tableau, within the stain.
This is different than the often-promoted shock of newness.
The intimacy of this limitlessness floods the discretion of the
present, the way long familiarity, with a lover's face, for example, or with a city or a room, can transform the well-known
features in their beloved relations into a landscape that opens
to all possible sentiments and their extremes, this in a momen-
tary shimmering. The same sudden inflection can happen in
a painting. A minor mark or shadow on a loved surface all at
once becomes the key to a completely altered understanding
of an image. The contours of that otherness describe a passage
not towards fixity or any kind of firm, locatable meaning, but
towards all the potentials of admixture, the sensual forgetting
of the name, all of the previously unrealizable futures that
can flicker in a glance.

It was early evening now, not long from closing, the time when the museum attendants, dressed in their tailored black suits, grouping themselves first in pairs, then gradually in more numbered clusters, speaking quietly amongst themselves, moving still slowly but with a gathering purposefulness, begin to usher we lingerers towards the distant exit. I adored this transition. My pace quickened slightly, almost matching theirs, yet pointedly loitering a little, before this image and that, with a minor disobedience that they too seemed to enjoy and even encourage with their glances. I felt a vibration of excitement. Soon I would stroll from the cushioned silence of the museum into the cool busy evening, I would pause outside of several warmly lit cafés without entering, scanning for a small empty table, I would continue to the Latin Quarter without choosing any café at all, the river beneath the bridge would darken, splendid. I felt like De Quincey, seeking some northwest passage through the knotty alleys of London, suddenly finding himself on a narrow footpath through a man's kitchen. The motion of time in this intermediate zone called evening filled me with humming expectation and ripe perplexities. I wanted to both slow and expand the moment as I walked through the long galleries with their seductive antechambers, now swiftly, now haltingly, as if searching for a landmark.

It was at such a moment of quickening that I was seized by the resistant glance of a small, shadowed portrait. Sulky, guarded, her pursed red lips seemingly chapped or bitten, her light, slightly rosy skin absorbing some of the mauvish-blue yet warm oyster-grey shadows of evening – in her I recognized my own complexion – the girl wore a large-collared brown velvet jacket like a precocious prince. She had unbuttoned it at her throat to show a loosely knotted carmine-and-white scarf, which rhymed with her skin and the thick auburn ringlets that grazed her velvet shoulders. Yet these garments were suggested rather than depicted, the white scarf just a scribble of bright writing, the velvet a warm deepening of shadow, a burnished darkness. Murky lamplight haloed her – azure chartreuse gold – showing the centre part of her darkish hair glowing pink in chiaroscuro. Such tenderness glimmered through that parting. Her face still had the soft androgyny of the very young. Her gaze was a statement of refusal. I leaned in to read the title. It was a portrait by Émile Deroy, close friend of the young Baudelaire, the likeness of an unnamed street singer much fawned over in their bohemian circle. The museum label called her *La Petite Mendiante Rousse*. The image hung at the far edge of a gallery filled with Théodore Géricault's lurid fighting horses, and various dramatized abductions and struggles by Eugène Delacroix. All the violence and perturbation of those paintings was met by the intensity of the brushwork in the girl's face and suggested garments. The surface of Deroy's portrait was in a vivid state of continuous expression.

Deroy had died at twenty-six, leaving only a few paintings, among them this nameless girl, and the only portrait of

Baudelaire in his grandiose moment, just before his ruin in the autumn of 1844. Deroy made the girl's portrait in '44 or '45, and then gave it to Banville, who hung it over his desk until the painter's death, when he returned it to Deroy's parents. The two young men had in fact met by means of this portrait, which for several days Banville had admired hanging in a shop window in the Latin Quarter, returning often to gaze at it. Abruptly one afternoon Deroy appeared and, without even introducing himself, insisted on offering the small canvas to the infatuated poet, who would just a little later encounter Baudelaire in the descriptions of their mutual friend Jeanne Duval. That same year Baudelaire dedicated a poem to the portrait's subject – 'To a Red-haired Beggar-girl' – and Banville and Dupont did the same with poems of their own. But she wasn't a beggar, she wasn't mendicant, she was a street singer. She frequented the Latin Quarter, where she played in doorways and squares. There was no shame in her calling. Singing was a public art; very often street songs were political and social commentaries, an unofficial form of broadcasting. Very often then the Irish plied it. Maybe she was Irish. It was the era of the potato famine, and many refugees scratched out a living in Paris. In all likelihood this girl was fetishized for her colouring. Red-haired prostitutes were highly valued then; the Goncourt brothers, in their diaries, delighted in describing the skin tone of red-haired women's sexes. Oh men. Our red-haired twats and our torn skirts, you must claim them. We sing anyways.

Perhaps this singer sat for the little circle. They collectively adored her. Perhaps they paid her just a little, but not enough to help, thus her sullenness and remove. Very likely she did not care about their ostentatious ambitions. She had her own songs. Or was there a little of the youthful camaraderie that can briefly bring together people of very different fortunes for a moment of struggle, of refusal? Had she been their friend? Maybe the brown velvet jacket is not even her own; she had borrowed it as the light fell and coolness came. In Banville's poem he imagines that she wears a then-outmoded kind of jacket called a casaquin, favoured by players of the commedia dell'arte, a tightly fitted seventeenth-century style, cut away at the bosom, flaring out from the nipped-in waist. She is said by Banville and Nadar in their memoirs to have played the guitar and sung in cafés, accompanied by a blonde girlfriend. These two were assumed to be lovers, which was a part of their erotic attraction. The Baudelaire circle – Nadar, Banville, Privat d'Anglemont, Pierre Dupont – relished these singing lesbians with their torn dresses, through which freckled skin would flash. Each of them described the red-haired singer, her skin, her garments, and her poverty, each used her as a mannequin for his sartorial fantasies. None of them named her. Baudelaire obsessed over the girl's tattered clothing. The ripped cloth was as luxurious as lace.

Pale girl with red hair
Whose torn dress

Reveals poorness
And beauty

To me, puny poet
Your young body, slight
Covered in freckles
Is the calling of sweetness

Formally the poem invoked the baroque poet Pierre de Ronsard, who had also written poems of this genre, the genre of the adulation of feminine poverty. Isn't all poverty feminine? They are tender men and they want to help, they say. Yet Baudelaire's poem was also ignited by an odd identification. He too, 'puny poet,' was now penniless. He could not have the girl because now that he shared her poverty, he couldn't buy even the cheap little trinkets he thought she wanted. He had no control of his future either. Now both street singer and poet were marked as outsiders. In the year of the composition of the poem to the red-haired girl, Baudelaire had half-seriously attempted suicide, stabbing himself in the heart with a little dagger at a cabaret, I repeat, stabbing himself in the heart with a little gold dagger at a cabaret, the dagger echoed in the poem by the glinting golden one he wished for the poor singer to tuck in her garter like a seductive jewel. Oh Baudelaire, you're pathetic, I love you. 'Go then,' he writes,

With no other ornament
Perfume, pearl, adamance
Than your slender nudity
O my beauty

She sticks her lip out and doesn't budge. The short life of Baudelaire, in its dizzying, troubled decline, was defined by the poet's self-recognition in the grotesque mirror of the social abjection of women. Whatever the red-haired singer thought of this, the men's aesthetic use of her person as a masque, will now be expressed by her resistant, unnamed glance.

SCENT BOTTLE

The prophetically dandiacal girl in her brown velvet jacket painted by Émile Deroy in 1845, the portrait of the nameless, adamant street singer, is the figure of a magnificent impulse. Her turbulent face demands: how does a girl become what she is – with no knowledge, but all of her visceral autonomy? In her gaze I coincide with my own tradition. It is made of multiple times, like bodies. And yet those bodies are now mostly nameless. In the shelter of this namelessness I have built various possible worlds – as many as I need. The girl made it possible to speak of myself.

I confess that the uncertainty that I felt at first has returned to me now in its full intensity. This cottage with its linden tree shelters a slow reckoning. First, I knew nothing, then I believed anything, now I doubt everything. Therefore I can invent. I thought that solitude was a necessary armour. I thought that freedom was a choice one made, a choice towards sentences and pleasure. I never once thought about fate. Now I know less. Now I think about anger. How does it work? Liver? Heart? Brain? I think that the evasive part of language is the materia medica of freedom.

To remember we're just clay, we're pigment, as we're being it, this is the great immodesty of art. I had a fundamental greediness for this immodesty. It radiated an attractive muteness, just beyond my cognitive limits. Materiality is too mild and limited a term for it. How to describe the sensation? Sometimes you shiver or shudder slightly, the instant before entering a room. Your approach has animated a spiritual obscurity. This bodily hesitation is a tradition, the tradition of entering the negation of names, and it colours the way I perceive all transition. Your body can sometimes deter its own representation; this breach indicates an interiorized covenant or constraint. It's called the feminine. It's a historical condition. The movement of perception or description, which are so closely intertwined as to be indiscernible, is not between nominal categories or aesthetic concepts. The girl is not a concept. Her idea has no core or centre; it takes place on the sills, in the non-enunciation of her name. This feminine namelessness seeps outwards with undisciplined grandeur. The girl's identity is not pointlike, so it can't be erased. It's a proliferating tissue of refusals. Unoriginal, it trails behind me, it darts before me, like my own shadow, or a torn garment. I say unoriginal because once she *was* named. The removal of her name is an historical choice, so ubiquitous that it seems natural. There is no nameless girl. There is no girl outside language. The girl is not an animal who goes aesthetically into the ground, as many of the philosophers would have it. The girl is an alarm. Her lust is always articulate. If her song goes unrecognized it's because its frame's been suppressed; her song is enunciation's ruin. It is a discontinuous distribution, without institution. Always the tumult of her face is saying something to her world. Prodigal, undisciplined, with an aptitude for melancholy and autonomous fidelity: nameless girl with your torn skirt, there's nothing left for you but to destroy art.

That is what Baudelaire wrote of young girls in his intimate journals: *The girl, frightful, monstrous, assassin of art. The girl, what she is in reality. A little lush and a little slut; the greatest imbecility joined with the greatest depravation.* I read this and then I reread it; I recoiled, predictably disgusted. Already this sort of cruelty had become familiar in my reading. Very often a text contains its own police; the she-reader is simply shut out, among various others, none of us the men of the declared inside. I read this excision everywhere. I read it in philosophy especially but also in poetry, in criticism, in history. The female is identified, then transformed to her predestined use, which is nameless. Any reader pertaining to the feminized category receives a gut punch. *Would you care to be prostituted?* Since I first began to read, the punch had been one part of reading. I felt it personally, that is to say, physically. Sometimes I braced myself and continued, bristling with cautious defensiveness. Sometimes I weakened and cried, ashamed even of my weakness. I believed it was my task to harden myself and persist. But gradually now the Baudelairean rant against the girl began to work differently in me. This slut insinuated attractive possibilities. What if this was not a punch but a perverse invitation? The lush imbecile beckoned me in. She begged me to become something. I paused, then I became that monster. I even expanded her grotesque domain, following the useful suggestion of Michèle Bernstein that it has become time to 'unleash inflation everywhere.' I followed instructions. I was obedient.

The aptitude for identification had been trained into me, I was made for it. My cathexes were the standard ones, and they were thorough. I was a girl. I entered literature like an assassin, leaking, fucking, wanting, drinking.

I did want to make art, but I, Hazel Brown, decided to make art by destroying it. The desire to write, to trace these monstrous figures on the ground of unprecedented longing – what is it but destruction? It produces nothing. Everything I was raised to be, all the docility instilled in me, the little punishments and constraints of girlhood, the intense violence and violations of adolescence, the roughly incised, undying shame of female maturity and fungibility, everything about my past and my ordained place in the world, which I tried to escape by constructing an autonomous world within the shoddy, inadequate confines of my room, my diary, my knowledge, all these things continued to live in me in the form of grave spiritual contradiction. I say contradiction, when what I mean is sickness. To write was to destroy something. I saw it everywhere. My girlfriends had scarred wrists and wept loudly and publicly. I would leave a trail of stains behind me, I would ooze out stains on my lovers' sheets, I would bleed through fabulous dresses, my thighs would be streaked. I would glance backwards looking for traces. I too wept copiously. The poets I read passionately wrote themselves into death, booze, disappearance. I too would drink. What else was there to do? The ancient refrain of weeping and drinking, the popular refrain of the negation of the desiring girl, it had to be violently seized, just the way my body had been seized, from behind, anonymously in the street at night, and flung against a wall. I had to destroy art in order to speak my monstrous life.

I believe this. I believed it then. How could I make it work? What were the terms of the violence I could own? The anonymity, the fungibility, this was a kind of cover, I thought, although now I doubt the tidiness of this inverted logic. Can disappearance create appearance? The anonymous girl was nobody, she was depraved and abject and so she could begin, I thought. There wasn't a way to dissuade her since she was invisible. But what was to begin? With all of her predecessors erased, how can she recognize her tradition? To begin was an internal attack on the feminine constraint. I decided that to begin was my calling. I was bad at it, which would be my foundation. Repeatedly I prevented myself from submitting to the minute internal transition, that mystic and terrorized transition between muteness and expression. How could I invent my self-education? *I know a young person who learned to write before learning to read,* said Rousseau, discussing the education of the girl, *who began to write with the needle before writing with the quill. Of all the letters, she first wanted only to make O's. She incessantly made big and little O's, O's of all sizes, O's inside one another, and always drawn backwards ...* In retrospect, I read in Rousseau an inadvertent formula for the solution I had stumbled upon more arduously, in piecemeal increments, through the many rooms, the many inhabitations and seductions, through the fucks that were mistakes. Reader, you must turn your depraved anonymity into a decor, O's within O's within O's, and within this baroque device, this carapace, exuded stitch by stitch, the drama of your moral self-invention will advance. I would discover the ornament of excess; there I would be schooled.

Now I think that girlhood in itself is a baroque condition.

When the Irish actress returned to rue du Cherche-Midi, I moved on to another room, this one also a seventh-floor chambre de bonne reached by a another dingy back stair, but in a more elegant neighbourhood, near the Parc Monceau. It was owned by a graphologist of popular fame – she had a radio program where she analyzed intellectual celebrities by means of their autographs. Before she accepted my damage deposit, she assessed my own self-conscious scrawl. I had met her in the bookstore where I used to linger at evening. I can't recall the sample sentence she asked me to copy out. Let us say it was this: *As for the seduction of the game, what if it is indifferent to us whether we win or lose?* The condition of transcription seemed unusual, but no more so than any other of the agreed-upon daily rituals I awkwardly attempted to reproduce. I suppose I passed her little test. This room, deep and narrow and dim like the last, had the almost shocking luxury of its own hand basin and water heater. There was a small window, an adequate bed, a chair, a narrow brown formica folding table, and a wardrobe. These were the graphologist's cast-offs. I recall a gently buckling faux wood-grain linoleum on the floor. I stored my books and my wine in the wardrobe with my few clothes. I had a bottle of Youth-Dew perfume from Estée Lauder, a gift from my grandmother, and I still associate the room with the heavy, pungent scent of civet and rose and clove. She had sent it in a little string-tied parcel, wrapped protectively in fragments of tissue-paper sewing patterns, the black outlines of the garment parts carefully clipped to include the graphic tabs that showed how to bring the fragments together to make a whole: a dress, a jacket, a new, better-clothed life. Always now the thought of the perfume in its cheap fluted glass bottle with gold paper label brings me back to that shitty room, its darkness, the blue typewriter on the folding table, the bad linoleum, these traits a carapace camouflaging a small freedom that gently expanded inside me like a subtle new organ, an actual muscular organ born of my own desire for what I took to be an impossible and necessary language. Its sillage was an architecture.

I remember that the beige wallpaper was embossed rather than printed, with the pattern of wicker basketry. Above my table, bordering the rough diagonal shape left by a torn-off shank of that paper, I tacked up three black-and-white post-cards: August Sander's 'Secretary at West German Radio, Cologne,' from 1931, her crisply shingled modern hair, ciga-rette, and aloofly hunched posture somehow at odds with the shiny black embroidered dress, which seemed to me to have been borrowed or handed down; Colette in middle age, leaning quizzically to one side, her glittering eyes heavily outlined in her signature kohl, in the foreground a large bouquet of out-of-focus dahlias; and a studio portrait of an elderly and monastic Georgia O'Keeffe, her grey hair tightly pulled back, and her black kimono-like jacket showing a crisp edge of white shirting. Like the street singer, the secretary was nameless. She had become her function. The part of her that refused this calculation held a cigarette. I found the three postcards very pleasing; I admired the effect of the diagonal, staggered line of small black-and-white images, which articulated the room's poorness. Also, though, I wanted to be witnessed. I considered that these three would help me to think. Influenced by the image of Colette, by Steichen I think, I sometimes bought tulips to put in the tall waterglass, and they would splay out and downwards on their long, weak stems, grotesque beside the bed in the dim light. I would take black-and-white photographs of them, a little blurred by long hand-held exposures. That spring I put tulips in all my poems. They were fists, they were cunts, they were clocks.

I found another menial job. A bourgeois man, a father, had approached me in the bookshop with an offer. It was the winter that I liked to go to the café to order port in its thick little stemmed glasses. I was slightly tipsy and I accepted; it felt so buoyant to say yes. I was to collect his young daughter from Hebrew school, take her home on the bus, and cook her lunch. There were two soldiers holding machine guns flanking the school's entry, which was at the rue Copernic synagogue, and I was to tell them a password in order to enter. I did not note it in my diary, but I wish I could remember it now. There had been a terrorist bombing five years previously at this synagogue, in 1980, and five people had died, and forty-four were injured, just as two years later there would be an attack killing six and injuring twenty-two, with machine guns and a grenade, at Goldenberg's, the Russian deli in the Marais where we would go to drink little icy vodkas with pickled fish. A year after that, a bomb killed five and injured fifty-one outside the Tati discount department store on rue de Rennes, the one where I bought a coffee pot and other small domestic items for my first room on the rue du Cherche-Midi. In that year, 1986, there were two dozen bombings in nine months, in post offices, book shops, metro stations, and shopping centres, all with connections to southern Mediterranean politics. Some of the attacks were anti-Zionist, or anti-Semitic, or both, carried out by organized supporters of Palestinian national groups. Some were claimed by the clandestine anarchist anti-imperialist group Action Directe; others by leftist Jewish anti-Zionist groups. Still others were presumably executed as acts of retaliation for France's support of Iraq, by pro-Iranian organizations; this was the case with the Tati store bombing, when just before lunch on a school holiday, the street filled with women and children, bombs were thrown from a passing car into the crowds milling around the sidewalk displays of cheap children's clothes. In those years there was a quotidian feeling of suspense and alert. At the rue Copernic synagogue I waited with the mothers in the new foyer, which had replaced the bombed-out one, until the children came running down the stairs. The girl came to me and held my hand.

After lunch at the family apartment I was to do the ironing and dusting while the girl played quietly. The linens would be dampened and rolled, waiting for me in an unused bidet. I was not bad at ironing. This was a household of dinner parties, so always there were napkins and tablecloths to press. There were ladies' blouses; the mother had gone back to work. I was here to replace certain of her domestic functions. Later, reflecting on my career in domestic labour, I would realize that the wife's role in the bourgeois household was so vast, so specialized, thorough, complex, and ornate all at once, that no single woman could perform the entire task. So the role of the wife was spatially distributed amidst an expanding circle of other females, some amateurs, some specialists, some fakes like me. We were paid for it, but not much. This was a household too of rare books, first editions, of collections of crystal paperweights and deep vermillion carpets. There was asymmetrical modern furniture that left me uncertain where to sit. Now I think that the strange and wonderful settee resembling a vaulting horse was by Zaha Hadid. I would polish the crystal glasses the mornings after dinner parties while reading pages of Richard Aldington's Boccaccio, thinking it rare. There were painted life-sized stat-ues of mythical animals, and papier-mâché statues of shoeshine boys; there was a large fish tank with an eel-like creature crawling along the fine gravel at the bottom. This fish tank cast a dull greenish light that still dominates my imagination of that apartment and its relationships. The grey-blue cat would crouch on the hood of the stove looking down as I cooked the girl's veal cutlet. The father boasted to me of his several mistresses, one of them, in London he said, with another child. As proof of his prowess he displayed to me the jangling keys to the mistresses' doors, which he kept in his suit's inner pocket together on a single fob. I would be paid 270 francs per week, he said. I could cover my rent and drink in cafés. This was good.

Sometimes the little girl's best friend would come for lunch. I would watch the two play together as I ironed. They wore tidy blouses tucked into stiffly pleated woollen skirts, sturdy shoes, and plastic hairbands. Sometimes they played chess until frightfully they knocked over all the chessmen and shouted and struck one another. They would erupt into jealousy at the lunch table; one of them said she would go for lunch *chez une autre copine. – Quelle copine?* Then ruthlessly tease the Burmese cat with its leash. The day before, the leash had been a harness, one girl the driver and the other the horse following commands, veering madly between the decorative papier-mâché figures. *C'est moi qui est la maitresse ici,* she said the first day I arrived, and she would sing children's songs in a high-pitched voice as I individually dusted the leather bindings of the books in the library. She would cling and kiss. When I read the picture book *Babar* aloud to her, familiar stories of elephants enacting colonial domestic rituals, she would fastidiously correct my French pronunciation, which was helpful. The lighting was kept very dim to protect all the rarity. There were special blinds. The girls played in the half-dark. Their games expressed all the muted power and violence inscribed in the rooms of that dark apartment, its objects and surfaces and collections, and also in the spaces outside the apartment, in the city; the confining luxury constrained them to play out the erotic catastrophes of their parents as well as family histories and political damages and hatreds that I witnessed in the streets. The collections made a decor of the undersides of these stories. None of us had any choice, neither the children nor me. Yet in a mild, non-committal way I disliked the children, and the parents, and my tasks. I did this sort of work because it was the work I had been raised to do, but I did it resentfully and badly. My gender, my poorness, and my foreignness were the job's only prerequisites. I was a sloppy, myopic domestic, one small component of the sprawling, mostly invisible assemblage known as 'wife.'

I would often be told at the last moment that I was not needed. Indeed I was very replaceable, not very serviceable. Other domestics would perhaps do their work more cheer-fully, more carefully. My permanent frown lines, heavy perfume, and tense, badly timed gestures disqualified me from seamless performance. I was often sullen. I had the wrong attitude, a condition that has apparently accompanied me for my whole life. Many have reminded me of this. 'The maid doesn't want to,' Sandrine Bonnaire slurs, playing the vagabond Mona in Varda's *Sans toit ni loi* as a profoundly decadent Bartleby. I would sometimes arrive at the apartment early, well before the girl's lunch, in order to take a clandestine bath, my own room having only the hand basin, and the concierge would notice, shooting me a look of contempt. I would often use my employer's better perfume, L'Air du Temps, reasoning that the bottle was so huge she would never know. I would sip from her crystal decanter of port at noon. I had yet to find a job that did not inadequately award my subservience. This made me perfectly feminine. Yet I had come to this city to appear to myself, to seek some kind of new language, not to iron tablecloths. I needed to keep this fact hidden most of the time.

The apartment was a scaled-down model of the city. Those tight rooms first exposed me to the domesticity and decor of wealth and the erasures and contradictions it masked. Everywhere there was damage. In the rooms filled with rarity and the dullness of familial hatred and jealousy, in the now-forgotten password spoken to the armed soldiers at the school, in the prying glance of the concierge, in the horrible statues of shoeshine boys, all of these things func- tions of varying scales of imposed and policed positionings of superiority, I thought I could intuit the whole sadistic spectrum of the political world. It was heavy with grief. This sensation was not aesthetical; it was the enforced affect of the sex of a political economy, of masked histories of colonialism, of the ugliness of wealth. My dream of grace, the difficult ideal I struggled towards in sex and in paintings, my unformed language for this feeling that was trying so mawkishly to become a life, would have nothing to do with what passed for luxury. But it couldn't be anchored by sadness either. I felt sure that beauty could only be slovenly and that love also could only be a slut. I suppose I simply reacted against the expectation of subservience. The only truth I knew was the truth of mendicant girls whose names were dismissed, the truth of linguistically fastidious girls who fiercely knocked over the chessmen and sang. I did not have to like any of it but I could admire their intrinsically exciting horseplay with its monstrous inner force.

CLOUDS

S lowly sipping a nourishing glass of beer on the terrace at le Narval on rue Saint-Jacques in late afternoon in the autumn of 1985 while reading the TLS: at this moment I felt like a gentleman scholar obeying the clock of ages as the marvellous clouds passed over. In the diminished scale of my economic existence, the beer could replace lunch, I'd discovered; the TLS could replace university. Wittgenstein, Guy Davenport, Zukofsky, post-structuralism – they each originated in those crisp, fine-set newsprint pages on a terrace. I could buy a fresh outfit if for a week I didn't eat lunch. I had a new teal-green suit I'd just changed into in the café toilet, carefully stepping out of my winter corduroys over the squatting hole before pulling up the slender skirt that at once made me feel like Colette. The jacket fell loosely from boyish padded shoulders to hips accentuated by the peplum-like flare of two diagonal pockets, and the fabric was a textured viscose weave that swung fluidly when I walked. It was an eighties vision of the forties, I think, by way of cheap Thierry Mugler or Claude Montana knock-offs. I took my place on the terrace. We were the clock, in our costumes and our habits, in our admiration for the simplicity of a system. There was a kind of nobility in it: insupportable nervous troubles, dusk, art, outfits, swiftening, disobedience.

The suit was a fictional garment that I liked to wear with a beret of the same colour. This green was the colour of my eyes in anger. When I say the suit was fictional I mean that it expressed one variation of a code, not to entrench me in a grid of meaning, as semiotic interpretations of fashion would have it, but to assist me in an unnamed metamorphosis. I hadn't then decided how to become that other thing, which here I will call for the sake of brevity a poet, but indecision did nothing to lessen my vehemence about it. I had not learned the ordinary, workaday devotions; I sought a mystic portal. I was practising versions of an intensity I supposed necessary to my ambition, an earnest desire that had found in Walter Pater a little ledge of language to perch upon for a while: 'to burn always with a hard gemlike flame,' as he said, in his conclusion to *The Renaissance*, 'a clear perpetual outline at the core of everything mutable.' I thought I'd find the gem in sex, this being an available mythology for the seeking and sensual girl. But mostly the fleshy tempests, which I had taken to be at the heart of my research, amounted to ornate flickerings. I began to suspect that, after all, such tempests were the grid, extending outwards in a metric repetition of the beauty problem that would permit only the most asinine deviations from the assigned roles in the drama. Next, reactively, I thought I'd found the gem in solitude. The word itself had a gorgeous, monkish allure. But what I called solitude lacked neutrality; it too was guarded by the stout wall of personality that I had no way of dismantling. Both sex and solitude fizzled with aphoristic recklessness. The strange perpetual weaving and unweaving of myself, as Pater referred to it, would continue. There was no one position that could reveal to me the seemingly occult passage to the desired metamorphosis; I had not yet discovered the innate monstrosity of pronouns, nor the freeing boredom of repetition, and what did I impatiently burn for? Something like an initiation or a revelation; to emerge one late morning from my chambre de bonne into a city that had overnight become the supple kaleidoscope of a female thinking. As it was, I made do. There was no dramatic metamorphosis, not that I could perceive in my daydreams or in my typewritten poems or in my diary. Yet in the city I was discovering, the collage of fantasy, pigment, quotation, and architecture that I walked through daily in my outfits and my obsessions, I came to notice small-scale transpositions, tiny openings within the texture of the present, where choices towards a freed thinking could be possible. Now I am not sure if these little tropes would be part of poetry or of philosophy. In truth I did not fully distinguish between the two; each was a baroque accretion of my body in the city. Doing philosophy would be the annotation of the present-tense irruption of my body in the city or in reading. Doing poetry would be renaming oneself as the heiress of a linguistic infraction.

The distinction between inner and outer worlds was becoming permeable and supple, like a fabric, which is in its very technical constitution both structure and surface. Painting, fashion, reading, dalliance: observing, and describing the surfaces of appearing, was giving me information about my mind and its desire. A movement in thinking was possible. Writing would be work that changed the rhetorical conditions of I-saying. My awareness of this soft border developed slowly, through error and habits of loitering, and yet I intuited it all at once, as soon as I arrived at the hotel called the Future. Both versions are true. How else does one know anything, except by simultaneous and mutually contradictory means? Like heavy silk, the inner world draped, folded, pooled, spilled over to embellish or seduce the outer world, which in turn frayed, abraded, tore, revealing the structure of the division as contingent, and so erotic. I was already becoming the city; when I went to look at paintings they were made in the same folds of light I walked through. The discretion of edges dissolved. My cognition moved more freely among the streets and bridges.

I'm thinking of Delacroix's little watercolour picture of an unmade bed as a diagram of this marbling effect. The tousled dull white glowing fabric of the depicted bedsheets, which, by the complexity and soft crispness of their rendered folds, appeared to be a heavy linen, or even, like the darned and mended noble country sheets one still finds in village sales, hemp, not recently laundered, held deep tarnished silvery folds and creases formed by the weight and movement of absent bodies. The flung-open coverings spoke of haste or at least carefreeness in rising, but no particular imprint, nothing that could be interpreted as a discrete sign, could be discerned in the fluent image. Even the little blue triangle of revealed mattress ticking, and beside, in joyous vibration, the vertical saffron-coloured bar of turned-back blanket – these hues anchored the composition in a vibration of carnal pleasure, not the fixity of a meaning. A horizontal bed plank and an aura or lip of smudgy shadow bordered this crumpled world. What I saw when I looked was a cosmology of tacit urgency that was also restful, milk-white into oyster towards lead, and that insistently yet carelessly extended beyond the bed frame, the tableau. The sense of languor and intimacy that emanated from the image was at once irresistible and completely impersonal. This intensely figured picture – for the folds were figural, if inhuman – did not require me to be anything other than a body with its timely weight and innate detail of proprioceptive awareness. No identity was necessary. I felt a restful stimulation, an alert calm readiness, and for the duration of my gaze on the picture's surface, nothing having to do with identity and its psychic and social constraints and fixations. (Searching now for the word *identity* in my miniature Johnson's dictionary, I don't find it – the 1832 text leaps from *igneous* to *jeweller*.) The image was a threshold.

I have said that the suit was knock-off Thierry Mugler, but when I bought it from a cheap boutique on the boulevard Saint-Michel I did not know of Thierry Mugler, and would not have recognized his signature cut, though it now seems so distinctive to the 1980s, bringing to mind photographs of the youthful Paloma Picasso, with her strong shoulders and angular allure. What drew me to the cluttered window where the suit had been dressing a dated mannequin was the piquant sense of the garment citing an earlier era, a styl-ized 1940s perhaps. This cut was familiar to me because of my informal studies in tailoring, recollections of old black-and-white snapshots of my grandmother and her sister arm-in-arm in the streets of Toronto, and also the postcards of Colette that I accumulated as placeholders in books and sometimes pinned up as modest decorations, as I have mentioned. Mugler had been citing an era forty years past, a time long enough to carry an exotic frisson, just as Deborah Turbeville, one of the compelling fashion photographers of the same period, whose images I admired in the fashion magazines that I browsed at kiosks and occasionally purchased, created a peculiar ambiance of suspended time-lessness precisely by combining what might have seemed irreconcilable temporal citations: her moody photographs had a Victorian daydreamt sensibility, where the tall, full-hipped models in their contemplative groupings seemed to bring Miss Havisham's wardrobe into the ruined bathhouses and abandoned country houses of the recent past. Here the 1970s cited the 1930s, which in turn referred to a mildly anarchic bluestocking nineteenth century. The clothes were those of intellectual governesses or defrocked nuns. Just where were the crumbling bathhouses? They seemed loca-tionless. They were unlike the scrupulously orderly public showers near the Pont-Sainte-Marie, where I would go on Wednesdays, meeting girlfriends, sharing our shampoo across the tiled cabin partitions, discussing philosophy in the steam, and where one could quietly tip the attendant in order to be permitted to clandestinely tint one's hair behind the closed door of the cabin. Turbeville's images posed silent women in ring-road landscapes, in abandoned ruins, among these the enticing ideological ruin of femininity, which had itself become a tableau vivant. The formally grouped models seemed to haunt their settings more than inhabit them. Were they not like Epicurean gods, caring nothing for this human mess, off in their separate realm of autonomous pleasure? These ruined bathhouses were psychic theatres for the illusion and disillusion of a dream of the feminine. If the models were to speak, they would repeat in monotones the words of Benjamin: 'There is no new style' or 'Even the most intimate idioms of the feminine are antithetical' or 'Truth is the death of intention.' Latent, passive, melancholy, framed by an architectural fantasy, Turbeville's female figures, both apparitional and absent, in the gently ahistorical commotion of their sartorial vocabulary, translated social mythology to artifice; they lovingly coaxed open the temporality of gender to erotically redistribute the image of femininity as a new baroque allegory. I understood this world. Confronted by the horror of gendered history, they prefer the architecture of myth, as I preferred my succession of dusty rooms. In the frisson of this redistribution, an ambivalent desire multiplies, plant-like, admitting bombast, distortion, awkwardness and incompetence into the mythic description. The women are monads.

The lack of authenticity of the green faux-Mugler suit, its obvious citational status, even the cheapness of its viscose fabric, which tended to stiffen and bunch up a little in the rain, requiring careful ironing to roughly restore its line: none of this offended me at all, contrary to the almost religious attitude regarding origin and authenticity that I still then fiercely cherished in all other domains of my experience, aesthetic or otherwise. The knock-off was a document and I was its historiographer, which is to say that in wearing the green faux–Thierry Mugler I became the historian of the present. The makers and distributers of knock-offs were close readers; they discerned the silhouette and the proportion defining the present almost as it was happening, just a demi-breath later, but before it became cliché. They sifted through a great many cuts and images even as they were being produced, clinically extracted and reassembled the essential lines and traits, dolman sleeve or drop shoulder or empire waist or elongated collar, to synthesize an ideal of a moment as it was passing. There are some poets of the knock-off and I refuse to scorn them. But Mugler himself was a poet of the silhouette, which is what made his garments so available for appropriation. He drew or rather projected an ideally androgynous stance upon a newly imagined city. His garments could change the meaning of a walk; they were a university of the walk. They gave the walker her setting and they gave the city the folds it had only dreamt previously. In the knock-off Mugler suit, through the medium of my stance,

I witnessed time imitating time and I liked it. Oh, I more than witnessed it. I wore mimetic time into the streets; I became its experimental body.

What I called sensibility in Turbeville's images, her soft-focus renditions of purloined novelistic scenes, the 'painterly' palettes, the self-sufficiency of the awkwardly posed mannequins, who seem to be collectively waiting for an impossibly distant event, intent on the expressive composition of their bodies with one another and with architecture, I might also call rhetoric, and this term could apply also to the seldom-addressed question of the social experience of wearing knock-offs. Whoever wears the knock-off cares very little about the reproduction of value, at least not in relation to the standard economies. Instead she knowingly inhabits a style of persuasion for the moment of its potency only. She puts her money elsewhere, if she has any. Rather than constructing a theory of fashion, she extracts an essence, a mythology of the instant, and applies it to her walk, her stance. The knock-off is tacky and won't last and it doesn't matter – it addresses streets and rooms in passing, like a mood or a crush. Gestural rather than narrative, it won't enter the archive. Wearing the knock-off, you have the full sensation of participating in your moment, like going on a supercondensed Grand Tour in 1759 without the inconvenient expense. It's an immersive form of research. This rhetorical gift, a form of illustrious sentiment, a livid vernacular, which is the knock-off's gesture towards the present, lifts and turns the body's experience of time, just enough to feel a psychosomatic rush. I liked to wear my green suit out walking, I liked to wear it to cafés after a long morning of sex, and I liked to wear it to parties. I liked to feel my gait a little transformed by it, I liked to feel modern, and in the theatre of the street, I enjoyed strangers' appreciative glances. I let my silk scarf ripple.

I recall one of those parties in a large and elegant Haussmannian flat on the Right Bank. I was buzzed into a tableau vivant of the fashionable and young intelligentsia. I had not been invited, but some of my companions knew the host, a chic young American girl who had come to do graduate work with Julia Kristeva. Who was Julia Kristeva? There was a special pause and hush around the uttering of her name, so I gathered that she was important. She had not been mentioned in *Structuralism and Since*, the red-and-cream paperback by John Sturrock, the one that told me all that I then knew about the Parisian intellectuals of the time. I had ordered it after reading a review in the TLS, and I still have that copy, especially foxed on the chapter dedicated to Foucault, on the front flyleaf the faint pencilled-in price of 72 francs. Since Sturrock hadn't mentioned them, I had heard nothing of the French Feminists until arriving at this party. The American girl, who I supposed to be a sort of heiress, by the grandeur of her apartment and the generosity of her bar, was bright and proud of her intellectual domain and she moved fluently like a seasoned hostess. I saw a lot of agnès b. at that brief and glorious moment, at the early cusp of spandex, when some intellectual girls liked to look like nineteenth-century parti-coloured acrobats. People were from Columbia and NYU and dressed down. I did not understand dressing down. In 1985 I thought Columbia was a country. I ought to have been more curious, but after kissing a girlish boy in the bathroom while teasing them with my vintage rhinestones, there was nothing left for me to do there. At this party, the mood of knowingness and understatement, as generalized as a decor, did not interest me much. I slipped back into my green jacket and I fled.

It was early October, a mild and clear night, and I walked towards the Pont Neuf with a feeling of exuberant release. What did I care about Columbia. The bridge was entirely swathed in a pale, softly glistening textile. I thought of Baudelaire's description of face powder in the chapter of *The Painter of Modern Life* that praises cosmetics – he said it created an abstract unity, like the tights of a dancer, transforming the wearer's flesh into art. The bridge was now art perhaps, thanks to its unifying covering; also, though, in a delicious inversion of the Baudelairean proportion, the bridge had, beneath the soft textile, become flesh, imbued with mysterious and occult passion. It was the subject of a wrapping project by Christo and Jeanne-Claude, and until that night I had only seen it from a distance, a kind of illustration of itself. The neoclassical pleating of its exquisitely cut cream-coloured bridge garment reflected softly in the dark river, and the tall lamps, veiled in the same textile, cast a mysterious light into the social night. Small groups of people discussing and laughing together approached the enticing monument, and we were welcomed by the genial bridge attendants, all of them dressed in well-fitted aviator-style jump suits of the same glowing cloth. It was a kind of synthetic from the future, with qualities both ancient and extraterrestrial. Very Issey Miyake, I'd now say, although at that time Issey Miyake had not yet begun to experiment with pleating. Swathed in its buttery pleats, the bridge had become an extravagant neoclassical breeze-cooled nightclub for anybody. Its flesh was collective. Each of the semicircular bays along the two sides hosted a small party. In these bays, the masonry was quite sumptuously and surprisingly padded or cushioned beneath the fabric, encouraging lingering, so people lounged and drank wine and talked and kissed. A familiar architecture had become a festival of pleasure. In the presence of the textile medium, newness entered a fresh constellation with the ancient. Near the Quai du Louvre on the Right Bank, the entire Samaritaine department store was also competently swathed, not in the creamy synthetic toile, but in a glittering iridescent plastic sheeting, in a pleasantly irritating promotional echo of art. On the Left Bank in the windows of the posh antique shops and galleries on rue de Seine, rare Venetian grotto chairs and gilded putti and candelabra were displayed in the vitrines, similarly wrapped in neutral cloth. Paris loved this. Why not, I thought. I was happy to enter the convivial night. The folds of the bridge fabric in the padded bays were as soiled and crumpled as Delacroix's unmade bed.

WHICH IS REAL?

Though I liked his philosophy of tailoring very much, I did not set out to compose the work of Baudelaire. In truth I'd barely read him. I entertained no particular literary nostalgia towards his canonical image, and I knew very little about his life. Between me and the Baudelaire concept there was no articulated relationship of influence, imitation, worship, or even rebuttal. When I think about the conditions of this involuntary transmission, although I don't believe that conditions are necessarily causes, I now see that I'd been nudged a little by the presence in my life of the worn yellow volume, and by the mostly passive absorption of a received mythology, as well as by the slightly more principled reading of a predictable cluster of critical texts, the ones more or less mandatory in my intellectual generation. Everyone reads an excerpt of *The Painter of Modern Life* alongside their Walter Benjamin and then moves on. Everyone reads three poems from *Le Spleen de Paris*. From time to time in my work I would use Baudelaire to explain a form: the relationship of the prose poem to the modern city and mass media, for example, as if any text could be tidily extruded from its social and economic setting. This was the kind of historical simplification that we called context. Maybe these incidental, dispassionate contacts with the Baudelaire material exerted subtle pressures whose import I didn't at first recognize, involved as I was with what seemed like more contemporary problems, such as the performativity of gender, or the politics of complicity. But I believe that there was no active sequence of cause and effect, no organic arc of development that could explain the transmission. I simply discovered within myself late one morning in middle age the authorship of all of Baudelaire's work. I can scarcely communicate the shock of the realization.

What then of this authorship, this boisterous covenant? I either received it entire, as one slips into a jacket and assumes its differently accented gestural life, or I uncovered it within myself, which is to say inwardly I fell upon it. I felt it as both purely external and self-identical. Perhaps these two things are not very different from one another. Life is apparitional. Fashion, as I have said, had initiated me into the untimeliness within the timely; after a period of forgetting, garments transcribe garments, unfurling a secretive negation within apparent semblance. We feel this slight vibration as the new. The art of psychoanalysis has demonstrated that a pure repetition of priorness *will* erupt in the present, so that the past and the present, for the potent duration of such an iconoclastic event, become self-identical, at the same time as everything will always not be the same, not being identical. Identity itself shelters or produces an Epicurean swerve. Repetition exceeds its appearance. I neither trust nor distrust the authorial repetition that I experienced; it has in me the status of a clinamen, beyond the mechanics of causation, which I can merely accommodate, however awkwardly. The stain of my awkward gender, my simultaneous embrace and refusal of girlishness, the untimely revelation of the Baudelairean authorship as purely girl, these burst forward as a turbulence in my experience of time, leaving me rawly susceptible perhaps. The girl within the Baudelairean body of work will undo it by repeating it within herself, as indeed she repeats girlhood, misshapen. She's always and only untimely, apparitional, forbidden, monstrous, a stain on authority. Her sensation is multiple, an intoxication of number. Only by the grace of this bulky untimeliness can the work resist all appropriation, reignite its innate obscenity, as the girl ignites her own obscenity as a form of freedom. But consider that the girl's obscenity does not always pertain to the recognizably sexualized categories. The terrain of the stain might be a wilful austerity, her withdrawal from the obvious rituals of corporal availability, in favour of the temporary privacy of a previously unintuited intellectual hospitality. I do think it was a kind of anachronistic hospitality that permitted the work's transmission, both my own acutely conditioned feminine hospitality, and the different but equivalent femininity of the Baudelairean oeuvre. This doubling dissolved borders. Desire flowered cognitively. Incomparably allegorical dahlia, recaptured tulip! The Baudelairean girl repeats her monstrosity for the benefit of a time to come. She will break open beauty and she will break open literature.

I'll explain again. Waking early one morning in a Vancouver hotel room in the spring of 2016, I picked up the copy of Baudelaire that I'd been up late reading the night before. It was a wide bed; I'd simply left the book splayed open on the other pillow and fallen asleep beside it as some might sleep with a cat curled close. I'd slept only lightly. I was preparing to teach a seminar on the prose poem, connecting Baudelaire's *Paris Spleen* to Rousseau's *Reveries of a Solitary Walker* and the *Essays* of Montaigne. I felt nervous about these intermittent teaching tasks and so I defensively overprepared; now those hurried studies haunted my sleep. Still in bed, barely awake, I clicked on the lamp, reached for the outdated dark blue Modern Library edition that had replaced the old paperback I'd lost. The translations were mawkish. The worn cloth cover felt comfortable and familiar. I read at random one sentence, a cry posing as a query:

Shall we ever live?

What happened was this: I smashed up against a violent and completely formed recognition that entered through my sleepy hands. The poems were my poems. The words as I read them were words I knew deeply because they were my own, the way my skin was physiologically my own. I'd muttered these words as I walked. I'd crossed them out after several years to replace them with other words and then changed them back. I was completely inside the poem I was reading, and also within its gradual, discontinuous making, which was both skin and breath, and too, sheer wit – no, I must try to be precise, it was in fact not a poem, but Baudelaire's preface to

the poems, written as a letter to his editor, Arsène Houssaye
– for I was starting once again at the beginning:

My dear friend, I am sending you a modest work of mine,
of which nobody can say without injustice that it has
neither beginning nor end, as everything in it is both head
and tail, one or the other or both at once, each way.

I was starting again at the beginning, which was an ending,
which was the middle of my life. I was not inside the meaning,
I was inside the words. I'd done nothing to merit this interi-
ority that was at the same time a superb exteriority, in just
the way that a word is at once both inside and outside, a
consciousness and a history, an urgent desire and a concept
originated by somebody else, if any concept could really be
said to have an origin – though I suspect that concepts are
collective habits in mentality. Furthermore, this doubled
picture is not enough. The mutability of the word as an action,
both emanating and absorptive, both willed and dreamt,
must be included. Any word I could think of was on the cusp
of a metamorphosis inaugurated by a single speaker's mouth.
In my unprecedented reception of the Baudelairean authorship, that female mouth was both his and mine.

Weren't all of my desires originated by an elsewhere? Isn't
this the structural experience of modern life? Such is the
Baudelairean proposition. The intoxication of newness is a
muted repetition. And we will lose sight of this elsewhere,

and then we will re-embellish it in the form of a personal myth. This myth becomes anyone's character, which is to say that composition presented to one's companions and bosses as one's being, out of the compulsion to entertain, or to be pitied, or to seduce. So thoroughly have we absorbed the truth of this proposition of the work of the elsewhere within modern desire that it has achieved invisibility. It is part of the language of the advertisers and the artists as well as the colonizers. The binary structure is theoretically convenient. Every city and every dream is erotically charged by an outside: a voyage, an ocean, a dalliance in a cabin, in a dim provincial hotel. Swiftly the voyage recedes. We forget who we were then in the haste to succeed at anything. We forget who we loved and who we fucked over. The forgetting comes to animate our experience of what we next call art. There is simultaneity within forgetting. Every line of memory twists back on itself, branches off, contracts and expands and repro-duces like a form of life. Now waking to the blue cloth book in my hand, the space of this potent recognition of a Baude-lairean infinity was electric in me. I was not in possession of anything. Even though I say that his authorship became mine, the possessive pronouns remain imprecise. There persisted between the two a gentle, even tender space. How can I describe it?

I recall a long afternoon kiss on the narrow cot in the maid's room on rue du Cherche-Midi. The shutters were half-closed and the light was vaguely green. My silk scarf covered the mirror. The boy wore a necklace, it was silver, I was naked, the room was cool and so was his amulet. He kissed me slowly up and down. Perhaps the little trinket was an ankh, a decorative sign some young men still affected in 1985, to signal sensitivity, I guess. This trinket, as he kissed me, trailed after his warm kiss over the surface of my body like a second cool kiss on its fine chain. Precise was the space between the kiss and the trinket. I felt the two simultaneously, although the warm kiss was the support for the cool kiss. Warm and then cool, though simultaneously warm and cool, I was only and ever the precise space between these two kisses, lust become artifice. The hospitality of the moving pause between the kiss and the necklace, pause where nothing happened other than the activation of my skin, the event of that caesura, the caesura that made of the afternoon kiss an augmentation I've carried continuously within me, as if on a fine continuous chain with no clasp, trinket forgotten for years, then recalled with the shock of an artifice that explains everything. Sometimes I did not like the love that I freely offered and received, and sometimes I liked it very much, as in the instance of this kiss.

This caesura inserted its livid pause in my thinking of words. Here I'll call it writing. But I wish to exorcise from this domain any assumption of authority. It is perhaps a false provenance, but I recall reading somewhere that the medieval Latin root of the word *author* was *auctore* – to augment. Not caring much for the scholarship of origins,

I've since held fast to this etymology as a truth, and not least as a method, without ever verifying it. To augment would be my work – to add the life of a girl without subtracting anything else from the composition, and then to watch the centre dissolve. It is exactly this sense of augmentation, which is to say, not necessarily an expansion or enlargement, but a timely complexification, sometimes an argumentation, at others a dissolution or the invention of a new form of refusal, that makes of the poem a possible space. The augmenter is the one who inserts extra folds into the woven substance of language. Extra to what? Certainly extra to the compact of the sign as the dual bearer of meaning. Each augmentation reveals that the theoretical model of the signifier and the signified will always leave something out of the description of language's dark work. The augmenter includes the displaced parts, because they are pleasurable, because they are moody, lazy, slutty, mannered, frivolous, unprincipled, because they are necessary, because they are monstrous, because they are angry, because history needs them without knowing it yet, because without them, the world gets grindingly thinner and more cruel, becomes a parody of the sign.

I have not taken this authorship and there has been no tiresome striving after it on my part: it has become me, as one becomes the finely drawn kiss one hospitably receives in a cool room, where the becoming is perceptible only because of the artifice of the pause between the kiss and the trinket, the pause's expansive, cosmetic generosity. I have said of my reception of the kiss that I was hospitable, because that is a habit of thought I bring to my consideration of femininity, and also to authorship, or to augmentation, as I prefer to call it, and I have said also that the kiss itself was hospitable, in that projection of reciprocity that temporarily annuls or disarms the strangeness and even the danger of sex, but now it is the cosmetic generosity of the doubled kiss, the infinitely unfolding generosity of artifice, which was not the boy's own generosity, as kind and as tender as he undoubtedly was in his boyish way, but the inherent and even unintended generosity of the structure of the kiss itself with its second trailing cooler silver kiss, which I must address. To have been thus doubly kissed, to have been drawn by a kiss, was a form of becoming. This kiss transcribed me. And yet for a very long time the double kiss had had to ripen upon me in its cool way, until in the morning hotel bed it awoke a second time within me, or indeed upon my skin, meaning also the skin of my tongue, as the artifice of my authorship of the works of Baudelaire. Between the wide bed of the hotel and the narrow bed of the maid's room on rue du Cherche-Midi, beds like two poles of a battery, the one with a book, the other with a boy, all of my life crowded, every part of the language that figured the pause that permitted me to enter poetry. Reader, I am sad to think of all the years that passed during which that kiss was forgotten.

The truth is, I only recalled the kiss because I had transcribed it. Even – or, I suppose, especially – the most delicately human truths can disappear. I had made a place for it then in the diary I have often mentioned in these pages, the heavy hard-bound diary with the brown leather spine, which weighed as much as a sturdy pair of leather boots. In black ink on blank cream-coloured laid paper, I had found a few phrases for the boy's kiss, for his silver necklace, for the soft light that afternoon, which was caught glinting in the necklace, in the midst of pages of lists and awkward drawings of coffee cups, park benches, and sculptures at the Louvre. This diary was a character in the drama I was constructing, the drama of my life, or at least my imagination of a possible and necessary life. It was my dirty and smudged receiver. Obediently it harboured the augmented kiss of the green afternoon.

I had begun the diary shortly before my first exodus to Paris, under the influence of my grandmother's death. While she was dying in a Toronto hospital I stayed in her apartment, a sparse place, since she had sold many possessions in order to get by. I took the bus to visit her every day, bringing her little puddings and treats to tempt her to eat, and a tape deck, so she could listen to music. I brought late Beethoven quartets on cassette. I applied lotion to her dry face and hands. I combed her hair. I helped her change her nightie. But what she wanted most from me, what she was hungry for, was description. She wanted me to describe everything to her and so I did: the route the bus had taken, the interiors of the various shops I visited, what trees were flowering and where, what I ate and where I bought it, how I had rinsed my blouses in the bathroom sink and hung them to drip dry over the tub. The vintage stay-up grid-patterned stockings I'd found in a vintage shop in Kensington Market. Nothing was too trivial. For my grandmother, in the last days of her living, description was a second life, a way of being in the world. It was what I could offer her, and it was what she could receive. Description soothed her. It was mortality's cosmetic. It enlarged the possible. And then, yellow with cancer, she died. I inherited the valise she had carried with her to the hospice. It contained an ocelot stole carefully preserved against moths in a cellophane wrapping, a stained mustard-coloured Schiaparelli raincoat, whose large cream-and-red-satin label with scribbled signature I have kept ever since, the prized raincoat itself long ago worn to tatters, and a pair of ebony cigarette holders. These items were the key to a dream of a different life. So I described for her. In this way writing became a magical procedure: describing the world in its smallest details was a work of love for the dead.

Now in this cottage in the middle of my life again I have been reading the rue du Cherche-Midi diary, and also the black one whose textured board covers are now fraying and detaching, as well as the smallish volume with better-quality taupe embossed linen binding and glossy cool white paper, mostly written in the summer of my servitude in the family summer house by the Norman coast, that house where the widow had told me that I was well-raised but not very clean. *Elle est bien-elevée mais pas très propre.* Well, she did not say it to me, she said it of me to a person on the telephone in a conversation that I overheard as I passed by the hallway telephone table during my morning tasks. That, too, I recorded in the diary. In this other diary, the leather diary of the rue du Cherche-Midi, I reread the kiss, and then in order to understand artifice, I inflate the kiss, I transform it to artifice, because I believe now that artifice is the soul, just as ardently as I once performed the quest for sincerity on the blank pages of the bound volumes. I'm rereading with an exemplary absence of system, a loose absence of thoroughness, in thready inversion of the method I had long ago brought to those pages. I used to want to describe every-thing, as I said, which necessarily caused imprecision. Yet the effort and striving, so legible to me now as I reread, yielded a kind of freedom, precisely in my inevitable failure to get it all down – the patterns of concrete floor tiles in 5 p.m. winter train stations lit by yellow incandescent light, the pink feather counterpane on the hotel bed in my room in Rheims when I went to see the twelve tapestries of the life of Mary in the cathedral and left with the image of bombed-out stained-glass windows incongruously pouring morning light into Gothic space, the riveting astonishment of the Cassavetes film *Love Streams* that I'd seen at a matinée on the boulevard Saint-Michel and left indelibly altered:

Gena Rowlands as the questing and numinous medieval philosopher of the expansion of love, her face like a bright planet across jittering chiaroscuro. Distant love, divorced love, mother-daughter love, rejected love, father-daughter love, sister-brother love, father-son love, human-animal love, polyamorous love, earth love, holy love, ludic love, experimental love, all splintered, imploded, swirled, marbled, leaked, knit in limitless kaleidoscope; the tenderness of the boy's gaze before he kissed me. Always there would be gaps in the description. In this way something indeterminate could flood in. I was looking for new life. I wanted to be as stupid as kissing, as dirty as a servant, as ripe as a blown-open diary, and I was.

Everything will fall short of the lucidity of this stain and its proliferation of vanishing points.

Also I reread to live doubly. I do now enjoy receiving the shock of audacity at the stain that I was. It is not possible that I was that girl, splintered, imploded, swirled, leaking, yet I hold here in my unmanicured hands her junky documents. Under their influence, I learn afresh the nobility of infidelity and artifice. Writing this now, or rather augmenting, for that is the action the doubleness incites, I feel a faintly obscene devotion to my own ridiculousness, as if I were a perverted naturalist describing a curious form of invasive vegetation. To everything I read in the diaries I now give the name *novel*, I give the name *knock-off*. Yet I am completely disgusted by literature. That's why this is erotic comedy.

A brief afternoon tempest; one petal slides under the door. The time of this cottage is kept in flowers. As a dandy fingers his lapels, I finger my book.

My dirty rooms, and my slightly dirty hair – for in 1985 I went to the public showers only weekly when I could not clandestinely bathe at my place of work – the musty or stale scent of my vintage woollen coat, which I covered over with the bittersweet religiosity of Youth-Dew perfume, these were marks of honour. The kind of writing I wanted to be would never smell like a literature of clean laundry, swept floors, and bars of white soap. My pens would burst in my bedsheets. My hair would perennially carry the sour odour of sleep. I believed that the poem must stink. Even reading the diary now I seem to detect the long sillage of acrid barks and herbs unctuously covered by vanilla, so that I am unsure whether years ago some amber drops of the viscous liquid actually penetrated the paper or whether my imagination produces this perfume as an insistent and elaborately feminine base note of reading.

Nadar said of the young Baudelaire that he poured drops of musk oil from a small glass vial onto his red carpets when he entertained his friends in his baroque apartment at the Hotel Pimodan. I had entered the musky sillage. The deepening life of reading was now the transmission of an atmosphere, a physiology of pleasure and its refusal or its augmentation by the several ghost-senses that moved between the phrases of a text. Some parts of this transmission would occur outside perception, but even the more overtly material aspects of the compact, the parts of meaning that filled the mind with grand glidings and swoopings and sudden small curls and dark retorts that were simultaneous, overlapping, and yet following one another in a sequence, like the completely absorbing and impossibly inventive movements of starling flocks across fields at dusk, even these parts would never find their completion in description. Always one part of the pattern would break off, glide towards a dispersal, sharply change direction, so that within a single murmuration several separate but superimposed fragments of the image were interweaving to briefly paint a density in the shape of a boot, a sickle, a leaf, a semicolon. Or, also like a semicolon, the curve of his necklace following the point of the boy's kiss slowly down the length of my body on the narrow cot in the maid's room on the rue du Cherche-Midi.

When later that afternoon he left my room, I reached for my diary and wrote: *The dear boy was nude, except for his speaking necklace.*

TWOFOLD ROOM

I left the selected poems of Algernon Charles Swinburne beneath the bed at what Paris hotel? Was it at the Quai Voltaire? I was there only briefly – a few nights at most. It was 1994. I had returned to my spiritual city, the city of my stain. I had reluctantly left seven years previously, intending to construct a less subservient livelihood. I applied myself earnestly to several callings, always bookish: copy editor, bookseller, research assistant, always as the general economy supporting the activity was in the course of being dismantled. So over time each experiment in practicality had foundered: there was nothing left for me to do but write. And so, this being my fate, I wrote ceaselessly. I went as far as I could into impossibility. Now at the age of thirty-four, with a plastic wallet of crisp traveller's cheques in my satchel beside the copy of Swinburne, I came back to look at Watteau and Boucher and to visit Rousseau's tomb. I had become obsessed with the eighteenth century, by way of a map that included nineteenth-century decadence, Virgil, Kate Moss, and Frank O'Hara. I had learned to use the word *research* to dignify such obsessions; sometimes I even said *lyric research*. What it meant was that I could continue drifting, learning how to describe the histories of surfaces and sentiments. I could return to the city that first received my fantastical project of becoming.

The tunnel beneath the English Channel had opened. It was the period of grunge and Comme des Garçons perfume, which I wore with fierce sincerity with my thrift-shop clothes, my Chanel Rouge-Noir nail lacquer, heavy boots, and very short hair. I recall that the room was very narrow, as was the bed, and that the wallpaper was covered in lugubrious yellow roses. Things left in hotel rooms: Swinburne, the moth-ridden morning jacket, a polished black teardrop-shaped pebble I had carried since childhood for luck, my Vivitar camera, my Canadian passport, my best brassiere, of magenta silk brocade trimmed in orange piping. Each of these items is now framed in my memory by the room where I left it behind, as if forgetting the object conceptually fixed the place and its decoration, in a perverse inversion of the often-mentioned technique of ancient memory. Here the object, the Swinburne Faber paperback, purple, absent, recalls the room, street sound and river light coming through the tall open window, and the heavy rosy Goth pulse of the amber scent in its odd flat transparent bottle. I had become an essayist. This meant that, rather than cruising the gardens, I directed my research towards the composition of highly decorative prose. What I had learned about borrowed rooms, wandering, and the receptivity of strangeness now shaped my sentences. Often I started out not knowing where I would arrive. How could I have anticipated, in 1985, sailing into the eighteenth century as if it were a harbour, as if I were the belated prosodist disembarking in a rowboat, clasping my little parcel of Vauvenargues and Sterne?

Beneath the city was an entirely different city. In Paris traces of baroque or mannerist lineage fluctuated like a network of nerve dendrons beneath the rational plan of Haussmannian capital. Ornate and discontinuous, this sensitive lacework receded into the obscurity of certain park groves, certain hidden inner courts, dusty service stairs, communicated glimmers of its electric substance to me in a diminished but nonetheless transformative repetition of the intensity that had come into full expression in Baudelaire, whose anachronous embrace of the baroque ideal of artifice was punished as obscenity. There could be no aesthetics of ambivalence in Second Empire Paris; capital's tenure permitted sincerity only. The sincere subject was governable. But beneath the city was another city, a place where monstrosity could find its double. Though here I have noted specifically abject sites overlooked by the fiscal overseers, this other city was even more potently a linguistic city, a gestural city, a city released from certain texts by their readers, as a sillage is the release of an alternate time signature by the perfumed body. No perfume, no syntax, no flower can be definitively policed.

Banville described with great precision and enthusiastic awe the furnishings of Baudelaire's Île Saint-Louis apartment, the one he was constrained to leave after his financial collapse. His memoir lingers on the ample divans, sofas, and armchairs, with their glazed cotton slipcovers (a textile then more typically used for women's petticoats and ecclesiastical undergarments), the glossy crimson-and-black-papered walls and antique damask curtains, so clearly influenced in their choice by Poe, who had recommended in his *Philosophy of Furniture* 'glossy paper ... with Arabesque devices of the prevalent crimson' and 'large low sofas of rosewood and crimson silk.' We read that, unusually, the apartment had no visible bookshelves, cabinets, or armoires: most of the young poet's possessions, including his surprisingly small collection of books – around thirty in number, and all finely bound (upon his death, Baudelaire was found to owe even more to his bookbinders than to his tailors) – his rare wines, and his emerald glass goblets, were discreetly stored in deep, hidden cupboards constructed within the remarkable thickness of the walls of the very old building. Such discretion was one facet of dandyism. But what impressed Banville most vividly about the furnishings was Baudelaire's immense elliptical baroque table, which was used, he said, for both dining and writing, and which Baudelaire always kept clear and uncluttered between uses. Banville attributed to this table's unusually irregular, whimsical form a sensitive power that inflected the body itself with pleasurable new abilities. 'Carved from solid walnut, it was one of those furnishings of genius, which we find in the eighteenth century, but which modern cabinet makers are powerless to imitate or reproduce. Indeed, its oval shape was endlessly transformed by inflections, apparently capricious and every-which-way, but to the contrary, the result of profound calculations. Not only did this ceaseless, undulating line seduce by way of its elegant caprice, but the table was contrived so that no matter how one sat at it, the body found itself supported, held softly, with no rigidity.'

Banville said that he believed the table itself was an element in the composition of *Les Fleurs du mal*.

In Banville's account of Baudelaire's baroque table, the object, with its insinuating, mobile edge, spoke through the soothed human body, which itself received, in its contact with this embracing line, uncommon compositional gifts. This was an erotics of furnishing. The body-table, for the two were joined in their mutuality by this transformative contour, wrote the poems whose serpentine address carved into and effaced the rectitude of the era. This combinatory, animistic formula found related expressions. For the poet, the discovery of the synesthesia of senses multiplied the powerfully resistant intelligence of metaphor: the image will always move just beyond any determining frame, according to an intensely evasive logic of sensual transposition. But there is also a related formal and tonal synesthesia inflecting Baudelaire's spiralling poetic line. The poems trace a turbulence that continued outwards, fractal, from the complex curvature of compositional time – a table in a room by a river – towards future contacts, future refrains, in infinitely productive tangents of temporal plasticity. A verse becomes a poem in prose; a youthful tenderness intertwines with and partly traduces future political despair. This turbulence reinvents itself in any reader as she leans into the embracing poem.

In considering the publication of *Les Fleurs du mal* and its subsequent trial, I believe it was the century that was obscene, not the poems. Baudelaire had composed a darkly fulgent antidote to capital's moral voraciousness, a homeo-pathic potion with a complex temporal structure, as the great noses compose noble perfumes based upon a necessary rot. Had the censors recognized the mortal danger to signification exuded by the infinitely proliferating folds and vortices of these flowers? They ravage all groomed certainty. The seduc-tive sweetness of the top note quickly succumbs to what we might consider the narrative components of the scent; this middle trajectory pretends to a functional, developmental sincerity, which it meanwhile viciously parodies. The final temporality is the lingering, superstructural one, a rigorous and beckoning decay deeply impregnating the senses, insin-uating its undesignated difference beneath and among the sanitized affects of the grid, the assassin of the very sweetness it had borne darkly forward.

The emperor and his crony Haussmann had attempted to entirely subject public life to quantification by a totalized power. They invented a terrible ratio: popular spaces, customs, and expressions, once policed, could be transformed to markets. By 1857, the year of the publication and trial of his book, Baudelaire's birth city had been appropriated to the new scheme. In Haussmannian urbanism, the grid in its vari-ous ideological manifestations cut through and replaced the winding entanglements of life and art and desire in the city. Haussmann's task was to translate Paris to an image of capital; the sites of errant subjectivity must be annexed, censored, owned. The popular, perambulatory trades of the streets were controlled by new systems of registration and censorship. This was a strategic annexation of culture whose purpose was to limit and eventually abolish the ungoverned movement of images, and their makers, across social and aesthetic borders. 'I detest the clockwork that removes the lines,' exclaimed Baudelaire in his poem 'Beauty,' with an audible sneer at the metric regulations of power. These lines are drawn and written, also traced, inflected, by meandering walkers, carved by baroque makers; they are rhymes, in the poetic technical parlance of his time; they are pre-metric units of human body measure; and they are the demoted lineages of baroque expression. Nothing disappears entirely. These are the lines that compel us to linger near fountains, to kiss strangers, to place an ornate pleasure at the secret core of our language.

Here I want to return to the physiognomy of inflection, the figure of the table becoming the body becoming the book of flowers. I have said that I've felt that it is the room that writes, that I simply lend it my pronoun. For Banville, Baudelaire's table was a linguistic force that collaborated with the poet's desire. The edges that separate things are conventional rather than inherent or inevitable. While it may make use of these edges in passing, the work of desire is borderless. Once set in motion by a site or an image, swervelike, the line of recollection simply continues, and in multiple directions, intensities, and temporalities, becoming surface, becoming ornament. I feel it in my body as I write this. The scent of a stairway, the glance of a painting and the eyes and the lips and the loneliness nonetheless. Here's a city that calls – be glorious fully in this poor minute. There is no unidirectional lust. We lean in and it careens to an elsewhere. It's both ahead of the body and behind the body, as well as all around it, like a voluminous shawl or scarf. Curves, counter-curves, folds entangle. To be held for an instant, to bring the furling velocity back towards the more limited scale of the speaker, desire seeks a language. The work of memory also enjoys the helpful artifice of a frame, a rhyme, a room, a table, a cartouche, a grammar. Desire and memory: their vertiginous animality is the condition of all predicates. Where would the dear bare body be without these ornate garments and phrases and ointments that bind us to time and each other? And so I wrote in my diaries to appease my fear of life disappearing, my fear of losing the stunning, grotesque ceaseless mixture of all of it. In continuing, in writing, my memory also twisted backward to transform the perception and interpretation of the image of my passionate concern. Was the boy's silver necklace an ankh? Were the roses yellow? Images and bodies interlace and resist significance. They'd rather exchange secrets. Meaning is inflected, multiplied, undergoes transformation by means of unchosen frequencies of similarity, projection, sensation, and intense emotion. Desire's logic is indeed synaesthetic. Biting hair, writing in water, naming god, perfuming the beloved, shaking cloth – the gesture is erased at the instant of its inscription, subsumed by the undulant inflection of an elemental embrace.

When I wrote sentences in my diary, willing myself to describe rooms, paintings, dreams, garments, encounters, and so to fix them against oblivion – crossing out and starting over, repeating, replacing and slightly altering, fibbing – I discovered that I wanted their edges to shimmer. I wanted the gorgeousness in the tawdry and girlish, but I also wanted the anger. Sentences had surfaces; I wanted them to begin to undo themselves, to career into the impossible. A sentence could be a blade. My task was to free the sentence from literature. To free it from culture even, since both are owned. At the beginning of my research I tested the potentials of duration in my diary, used the leaves of the bound volume as a laboratory. Never had a girl written anything long enough. If I could open the temporality in sentences, perhaps a transformation could take hold. It was the simplest idea, but had some inadvertent merit, in that it forced me to recognize time as a linguistic material. Therefore time did become my linguistic material. Patience and impatience intertwined in a lacework. Pattern emerged. I was no avant-gardist; I had no interest in abolishing grammar. Rather, I studied it, in a casual way. I wanted to understand subordination. I thought it could be useful. I dallied with additive phrases, internal digressions, parallel constructions, and deferred predicates; I saw that the shape of the sentence could be dangerous. Instead of accommodating and representing the already-known, so limiting identity and collectivity, this shape could instead become a force of inflection. Like the baroque table, like a spiralling scene in a movie by Cassevetes, at the core of a storm a dog becomes a blonde person who speaks soundlessly into the heart.

Outside my doorstep the rose thrusts up dark purple shoots, three or four inches per day, soundlessly into the heart.

The sentence: subjectivity followed by a pause. Subjectivity: whatever desires or hates. Now the pronoun could be limitlessly potent instead of retrospectively descriptive; the sentence, rather than receiving the dumb imprint of my always too-limited experience, could hold grammar open to future becoming, or shut it capriciously to evade determination. Now all at once I could recognize my own anger – it wasn't hot and explosive, but an ice-edged retraction. Often this recognition had evaded me in my life. I had felt that I had no anger until I took hold of that cold blade. I came to feel grammar as an elemental matrix. All possible co-mixture and variability came into being in tandem with the technology of those prismatic constraints. I say to myself in the pimp's room, Now Try to Have a Fucking Thought About Beauty. What future strangers would recognize themselves in this charged, citational, 'I'? What would a girl's anger be? How would each speaking girl transform her pronoun? It's a fractured citation. Everything that's ever passed through it has left behind traces of fragrance: coconut, musk, and fear. We speak the words others have spoken, in new settings, and so transform them a little, while the trace of the old speakers also remains active, moving into the potent future. The pronoun is just the most intense point of this timely reinvention. The feeling of having an inner life, animated by a cold-hot point of identification called 'I,' is a linguistic collaboration. We speak only through others' mouths.

This was frightening, to embrace the unacknowledged intimacy of linguistics, and so I continued the thought. By what profound calculations, as Banville had said of the design of Baudelaire's table, could the contours of the sentence be transformed, and what would I then become? Yet what I had already, coming to this table, was something easy and useful and fresh, and was given to me by sentences: the cool sensation that my body was already in the middle of thinking, and that this condition, in both its lust and its anger, was average, unremarkable, so free.

I would have liked my sentences to devour time. They'd be fat with it.

In what sense is anger ornamental? When it permits a girl to pleasurably appear to herself. There was never a room that could hold my anger and so I went to the infinity of the phrase. Obviously it wasn't simple like that. Anger was my complicated grace.

The sexuality of sentences: Reader, I weep in it.

DRUNK

I had been given an old school copy of *Les Fleurs du mal* by one of the Huguenot granddaughters. Its mustard-coloured worn paper cover felt like velvet. I was not able to actually read the poems but I very often looked at the printed pages, tracing the distribution of the ragged lines across brittle paper. I began to see the poems in their typographical arrangement on paper as kinds of portraits. They were portraits of poems, much in the way that, between exhibitions, in the temporarily emptied room of a nineteenth-century museum, the indigo or crimson fabric-covered walls will be unevenly faded, revealing the brighter shapes of pictures that had long hung there, as ghosts of previous syntaxes of display and relationship. These absent shapes were now spaces for thinking something new. Whatever newness might be – for now, like a geometer, I think there is very little that is ever new on this earth. What we name invention is mostly recombination. But then the idea of the new burned like a faith within me. After many years of such ruminations and countless moves between cheap rooms, I lost track of the book, whose covers had come loose, leaving the onion-skin paper vulnerable to damage. Still by the time it disappeared I had not actually read it, though I had absorbed it through my hands. My experience of Baudelaire was haptic. The granddaughter had also given me a paperback Littré dictionary, which I continue to keep on my writing table. It is the 1971 10/18 edition from Christian Bourgois and Dominique de Roux, with a glossy purple cover showing a slash of sulphur yellow and a disk of cyan, within which nested the stern photographic portrait of Émile Littré, the theosophist lexicographer. Several children's names were written shakily and boldly on the first pages of the dictionary, in various colours of ink, accompanied by geometric doodles: Emmanuel, Jean, Caron. Inside, apparently random words were highlighted with yellow bars: *exacerber, pondereuse, protectorat, regressive, affecter*. It was the code to my future and I could not yet read it, or it was nothing, a chance scattering of various kinds of idiosyncratic marginalia – stars, underlinings, groupings of successive entries linked by soft vertical slashes in pencil. Next to *gambade* is a small black ink drawing of a crystal.

A gambade is a caper, a frisk, a prancing. It is also the successful evasion of the payment of a debt, especially by a poet.

Around the time I lost the worn but unread copy of *Les Fleurs du mal*, I found a tailored black mid-nineteenth-century gentleman's jacket at a flea market at Bastille. I suppose it would be called a frock coat, or perhaps a morning jacket. Its fitted sleeves were mounted quite high on the torso, its shoulders were softly rounded in an unfamiliar manner, and slipping it on I felt a freshened awareness of the articulations and expressions of my arms. I longed for a decorative walking stick. From a slightly accented waist its longish skirt flared a bit behind, encouraging a brisk, decorative enunciation of my step; this jacket added a grain of wit to its wearer's walk, like a mild sartorial drug. It buttoned to the middle of the breastbone, and the largish buttons were covered in velvet, which had frayed at the edges, as had the softly turned, broad and high lapels. I recalled the theory of lapels I had once read without retaining the name of its author: the lapel is a gentleman's expression of vulva-envy. The old jacket fit me perfectly. Wearing this garment transmitted to my own body a metamorphosis in corporal gesture; though my physique and posture were more accented than altered, my bodily vocabulary opened to movements and stances generally only intuited now with the help of old photographs, such as those by Nadar or Carjat. The tailoring of the jacket moulded a new gait, a new stance, a gestural etiquette. I say new because it was unique in my proprioceptive grammar, though in reality what I had slipped into was an all-but-vanished ethics of sensation. I felt a lightened precision in my movements, coupled with a pleasurable cast of subtle constraint. I felt the flare of my high lapels. I bought the jacket.

As I write this I recall the first tailored jacket I ever wore. I was twenty-one and had just vowed to follow this calling to the end. I felt that my vow merited some decorum. I went to a Vancouver department store – Eatons, in 1982 – bought a full-priced diary bound in a William Morris print, and the black jacket, heavily discounted. I have long since lost both. To acquire these items I used a department store credit card that I never paid off, a very useful tool that at various times also procured lingerie, cooking pots, and perfumes. My balance simply disappeared when the store went bankrupt in 1999. This, I suppose, could be called a gambade.

The first jacket had narrow lapels and a narrow cut in the torso too, in a slubby, blended fabric that suggested linen but wasn't; I wore its sleeves rolled to show the shiny teal-blue lining above my silver bracelets. This was the jacket I wore daily on my first trip to Paris. It served as a gateway drug to tailoring proper. I realize now that it cited the barest hint of glam. Several years later, after a series of thrifted stand-ins, I received my first writers' grant and I bought, late in sale season, an early jacket by the Belgian designer Ann Demeulemeester. The Antwerp Six were radiating abundant newness; all we read then was post-structuralist. Especially we cited and recited Gilles Deleuze's book *The Fold*, which had been translated into English that year. 'The characteristic of the baroque is the fold that goes on to infinity,' we solemnly chanted. The jacket was cut like a fluid black shirt that swung out from narrowly fitted, slightly moulded shoulders; this sensual belling effect was subtly accented by some careful structural facing at the inner hem, to sketch a slouching line that was unrecognizably fresh in 1994, when the mainstream of fashion still subscribed to the 'strong shoulder' of what was then called power dressing. The lapels were deeply notched and rounded, stitched by hand at the edges. I wore it with everything for years, as others might superstitiously wear a fetishized pendant or a ring, believing in its influencing attributes, and in fact this jacket made the most haphazard T-shirt, the most lovesick bad mood, into a knowing statement. Although it was perfect over long grunge dresses and tattered bias-cut skirts, I especially wore it to write in, over silk pyjamas, feeling like a mildly Goth Sacheverell Sitwell. It seemed obvious that this jacket would write rigorously fluid, decoratively melancholic poems, and it did. I still keep the Belgian jacket, now with wilted lapels and gaping pockets, the light wool crepe fabric gone shiny at the hip where my satchel rubbed, with a feeling of gratitude as well as a sense of ethical responsibility to the preservation of an alternative history of tailoring. It was followed by an oddly puckered wool-and-nylon bolero by Comme des Garçons, found on eBay, this one with a stiff wide body and a high round collar that stood out from the collarbones like an early Balenciaga (the inside as the operation of the outside, croons Deleuze), then next another Comme des Garçons, with knitted sleeves that ended at the elbow, and a long, tightly ruched waist in a dense gabardine that gave to the proportional play the backbone of Saville Row. I had had a complex, night-long dream comparing Rei Kawakubo to Elsa Schiaparelli, which led, just as I woke, to the gnomic and lapidary statement *Rei Kawakubo takes the politics of freedom seriously*; for years afterward I searched assiduously for her gorgeously monstrous garments in consignment shops and thrift bins, with only minor success.

All of those jackets I wore over anything at all during the long era of intensive feminist theoretical study; they accompanied my ardent forays into Donna Haraway's *Cyborg Manifesto* – for indeed I was no goddess – and the world-changing texts of Judith Butler, the shockingly liberating *Gender Trouble*, for which Foucault's work on sexuality had begun to clear the way, as well as the denser, more philosophically challenging *Bodies That Matter*, which displaced the habitual feminization of materiality in favour of a rigorous historicization of concepts. 'The category of women,' she wrote, 'does not become useless through deconstruction, but becomes one whose uses are no longer reified as "referents," and which stand a chance of being opened up, indeed, of coming to signify in ways that none of us can predict in advance.' I craved the unpredictable spaciousness of this opened-up category.

My most recent jacket, entirely worthy of this thrifted lineage of radical women tailors and philosophers, is by Limi Feu, the daughter of Yohji Yamamoto; I discovered it on eBay for forty euros. My heart is fire, she says. It's double-breasted – my first ever double-breasted jacket, I should add – also in black gabardine, slightly cropped like a little sailor's peacoat, edged down the high, wide-ish lapels on either side with a raw line of glistening tar. The armholes are cut close to the torso and the quite long sleeves end in belling cuffs, bordered also in tar. I say tar, realizing it is probably some sort of acrylic medium, but the effect is tar to the point where, wearing the jacket, one imagines its penetrating and dusky scent. The jacket's back, rather than having the conventional small vent for ease of wearing, is aggressively slashed up to the shoulder blades, to reveal in a narrow vee, beneath the tarred edges, the wearer's shirt, white and rumpled quite likely, or to expose bared the skin of the her back. This jacket has tempered my readings of Giorgio Agamben with an insouciant skepticism; it is of a spirit perhaps, with Sara Ahmed's phenomenological queering of geometry. 'What lines,' she asks, 'will cover the page when the woman philosopher inhabits the space by the writing table and takes up her pen?' These garments, accompanying me in heavy, oversized suitcases or following me more recently in my movements between continents and academic residencies by slow-shipped container, form a geometry of thinking. Only the first one, the skimpy citation of glam by the now-disappeared T. Eaton company, has been lost.

At the Bastille flea market I did consider, to the point of active belief, that my newly acquired garment was Baudelairean; how many times had the poet visited his clothier with a subtle vision in mind, worked together with the patient tailor through many fittings and small alterations to achieve the vision, and then, very soon after leaving the shop with the beautiful garment, not having yet paid for it (since still in the early nineteenth century convivial neighbourly relationships with tradesmen were structured by means of credit), next have to pawn it, receiving some insufficient sum to keep at bay the antiques dealer he owed for a forged Poussin, or to partly pay off the hotel keeper, to avoid having to leave the shabby establishment under cover of night, leaving behind important books and prints and manuscripts – maybe even some drawings by Constantin Guys – or to appease the pharmacist for the medications that failed to heal his venereal disease, the opium that failed to calm his chagrin? There had been so many Baudelairean jackets, each part of the infinite cycle of clothing, pawning, borrowing, owing, which, continuously recombinant, functioned in his life as the cardinal directions or the cosmic elements did in ancient geometries. Surely some of the purloined jackets were still circulating in the rag cosmos. The poet was not alone in upholding this sartorial cosmology. Marx, too, while writing *Capital* in London, rhythmically pawned his coat and then borrowed to retrieve it; so determining was this mobile garment and its liquid value that he used its image to begin the great study of the production of value in modernity. 'A coat is a use-value,' Marx wrote, 'that is determined by need.' It was said that he could only go to the library to research his lifework on those days when his coat was out of hock. At such times Baudelaire, or so he wrote to his mother, seeking yet another small advance on his capital to again renew the cycle, would wear all of his shirts at once and not go out. So the coat was also a fungible money – at the pawnshop it represented to its temporary owner not its usefulness, but a mobile unit of value in itself. A coat became heating wood, coffee, a room, time.

Jackets and coats are awkward to pack in suitcases. If the season changes just as one moves on, often a jacket will be left behind, along with several books. What happened to my wide-collared late-1940s greatcoat, the one I wore with jazz shoes to cruise in the Luxembourg Gardens? After only a season of wear I had had to leave the fortuitous garment in one of the bare hotels, its lining torn to ribbons and the edges of the wide cuffs frayed, but I had loved that coat and the heavy swish of its hem above my ankles in the public gardens. When I came to this hamlet, dragging my huge suitcases over the threshold, I had not been able to divest myself of the collection of Japanese tailoring I had gathered over decades with the ritual secrecy of a committed addict, nor my collection of red-and-green Loebs in their bright and plain paper covers, nor my early diaries. This cottage is now my archive. I am not sure that this is what I imagined for my life in poetry as I strove away on my blue typewriter in chambres de bonnes in 1985, yet having achieved such an archive I am not dissatisfied. In melancholic moments I refer to it as my hut, as it is very cheap, sparsely furnished, uninsulated, and heated by one wood stove. Many would consider it unsuitable for habitation. I can say that it does not leak. But if it is a hut, it is a dandiacal hut; all of my early urban fantasies, sartorial, perambulatory, philosophical, are now concentrated in its rough rafters and stone walls. My walks with my dog through the fields are theoretical experiments in the association of arcane concepts with a material history of margins.

The landscape itself rhythmically conceals and reveals a tracing of the seizure and scarring of the earth by capital. Here I am not so much a recluse as an archivist of the ephemeral. This is one possible fate for the female thinker; this is one of the calmants of my heart.

I went to Sheffield, wearing the Baudelairean jacket. It was an extremely mild and grey day in February. I travelled northwards by train from Paris. I wore no overcoat, just a loose and long white cotton men's tuxedo shirt beneath the adored garment, whose breast pocket I had decorated, just the month before for the New Year's festivities, with a flesh-pink silk pouf. I felt very dapper. I wore my now-greying hair in a loose pageboy and my fingernails habitually painted with the Chanel Rouge-Noir nail polish that I had begun to fetishize the moment I became aware of its existence, which coincidentally was the year I published my first book, so that always now I associate this high Goth colour with the thrill of first publication. I improvised a sort of cravat from a tatter of black lace. I would tell no one that my outré jacket was Baudelairean, preferring to keep private that part of my poetical fantasy. I carried only a small satchel, with some personal items, and a few copies of my book to distribute among my hosts. I was not staying for long. I would need no other costume.

I made my way to London, then paused there for a night. I was to stay with a friend and visit the Joseph Beuys exhibition hosted by the Tate before continuing on to Sheffield the next day. We were at this exhibition, my friend and I, discussing Beuys's seriously ridiculous installation *The Pack*, in which a fleet of wooden dogsleds tumbles outwards, bearing grease-farded grey felt cargoes, fanning from the opened rear doors of a Volkswagen van, and as we rehearsed our reservations about Beuys's shamanic proclivities, barely conscious of my gesture, I reached for the pink silk pouf to clean my glasses. From the breast pocket of the Baudelairean jacket, following the small flourish of the pink square, escaped a stream of small moths. Softly they fluttered over the dogsleds with their rolls of felt. Do moths also go for fat? I thought it was my own heart that was moth-ridden, such deep mortification did I feel, and when later we returned to my friend's house, I hung my jacket outside the front door on a shrub, not willing to infect her elegant premises with my travelling scourge. I had already inaugurated the destruction of the part of the heritage of Joseph Beuys that was made out of felt, but at least my friend's own tailoring and upholsteries would remain intact. The next morning as I left, I retrieved the jacket from its branch, and with an appalled awareness that the garment I wore was in fact alive, and exactly why it had been so cheap to buy at the usually bourgeois Bastille market, I continued to my destination.

In Sheffield the conventional pleasures of the experimental poetry event awaited. I was met by my hosts at the train station, itself a very Goth, worn-out fantasy with its rusting lacelike steel skeleton and expanses of roughly boarded-up glass between faux-medieval masonry arches. A thatch of bright band posters covered the hoardings and yellow-and-black emergency tape cordoned off the most decrepit parts of the station. There was garbage loosely heaped everywhere and several interior sand piles; the visual and spatial complexity was so absorbing that it was difficult to locate a door. The systems and infrastructures were continuing to erode, as they had been doing since the arrival of Thatcher in 1979, and the defunct industrial beauty of nineteenth-century train stations was no exception. Everything had been privatized or was about to be privatized except for poetry, which was worthless. These things, and others, about the depressed local economy, the fall of the social state, and the increasing precariousness of survival, were explained to me as I walked with my hosts to the pub where the reading would be held. Emboldened by our shared contempt for capital and our appreciation for difficult syntax, we drank a great deal. Plastic cups of red wine stained our lips black. We continued after the poetry reading to an Italian restaurant, ate heartily, danced between the tables after closing, and then went back to the house of the hosts. By then drunk, I had forgotten about the shameful condition of my jacket. I flung it over the back of an armchair with everyone's coats, in a great dark tangle. We continued our drinking discussions.

Finally in very early morning it became time to leave. I had not yet checked into the hotel that my hosts had provided for my visit, together with a small stipend and the train ticket. Searching for my jacket among all the others in the heap of black cloth, I suddenly remembered the moths; I dissolved in laughter. When I explained my situation, my hosts recoiled. Like most poets I knew, they were great collectors of vintage tailoring and old cashmere and beautifully worn carpets and now I had in all likelihood infected their house. The more they recoiled, the louder I laughed. Nothing could be as ridiculous as this. I laughed till I wept. I would not be asked back. Tersely now I was accompanied to my hotel.

It was a sprawling, worn-out place just across from the train station, and had not yet been visited by the glitzy scourge of provincial hotel renovation – no eggplant over-scaled paisley carpet, no smoky-mirrored dividing screens in the so-called breakfast room, no chrome-plated light fixtures hanging from exposed, black-painted ductwork in great bundled clumps. Instead it was simply and reassuringly nondescript. Brownish, I guess. The desk clerk discovered that I was not in their system – my registration had been lost. And what was more awkward, the hotel was entirely booked by a stag party. It was very late at night, and we all searched for a solution. It was decided that I could stay in what the clerk termed the 'hospitality suite,' the only uninhabited room that remained, a room not typically let out for entire nights. It was on the ground floor directly across from the back entry to the bar. I needed very much to sleep off my wine, so I accepted the proposition. My host left, satisfied that I'd been properly seen to.

This room was very large, and judging from the state of the carpet, had accommodated its share of parties. There were cigarette burns edging the few pieces of formica furniture, and in the middle of the room, the sagging bed was covered with a pink quilted nylon bedspread that seemed to have been there since the year of my birth. Not caring to witness the bedsheets, I fell on top of the pink coverlet, still wearing the infamous jacket, and slept.

I dreamt drunkenly of the origin of tailoring.

In the quite late utopia of my sleep, a sartorial aura distributed itself across the long textile era called modernity. I turned on the pink coverlet. The mediocrity of capital was parodied on a lapel. This meant that textile's inherently mechanical reproducibility stretched in taut dialectic with the draper's fold, repeating and repeating and repeating. I threw my sleeping arm across a stain. A she-tailor sliced into the continuous cloth of capital to cut a garment. This garment constructed the pure ideality of the androgynous form. Who was this tailor? I muttered and scowled without waking. The tailor was modernity's mystic. I had not even removed my boots. She said that the tailored garment first developed in the Middle Ages as a fitted woollen underlayer for suits of metal armour. She said it was constructed in order to prevent chafing. Now my boots were chafing. She said that before the fourteenth century all garments were made of simple uncut squares and rectangles of cloth. The dream was very long. Now I was weaving rectangles. Folded rectangle was stitched to folded rectangle. All edges were woven selvedges. I kept sleeping. I kept stitching. She said that before armour the beautiful power of garments was the rhythm of folds. I felt the folded beauty in my sleep. She said that the folds were inconveniently uncomfortable beneath the snugly fitted armour. They clumped up and chafed and bruised the wearer. Therefore the tailoring or cuts, drawing the garment close to the living skin. One part of the technique of tailoring was layering many mitred woollen pieces to mould a form. The woollen layers constituted a padding fitted to the body. She said that in so contriving the woollen padding, she transformed the suit of armour to a kind of furnace or chrysalis. From it the dandy inevitably emerged. I was waking, still a little moist, coyly fluttering the tails of my morning jacket.

Sunlight penetrated the hospitality suite. There was very little time, no time for breakfast. I had to catch my train. My mouth was not a good place. I stank. Also my jacket stank. It had been through a great deal. I recalled the moths.

In the far corner of the room was an armoire. What did an armoire have to do with the sort of hospitality this room proffered? It was not even formica; it looked like walnut. It was decoratively crested with a carved geometrical cornice, and a tarnished key dangling a scrap of ribbon emerged from its lock. It exuded a magnetic force. I opened it. The interior was lined in peculiar floral wallpaper. It was as if this armoire had materialized in the night, transubstantiated from a cheap hotel on the boulevard de Bonne Nouvelle in 1865. I saw hashish-emboldened stories in the shapes of the flowers. A wooden hanger hung on a hook. Otherwise the armoire was empty. There only one thing to do, and I did it with a kind of quick instinct, as would an artist who all at once, in her studio, perceives the only solution to a long-standing, worried-over metaphysical problem. I removed my jacket and hung it there, respectfully and tenderly buttoning its buttons and adjusting the fall of the shoulders on the wooden hanger. I closed the armoire, then ran for my train.

This is how I lost both the poems and the jacket of Baudelaire, and in doing so made my only installation work. Perhaps the armoire has never since been opened, and inside it, the jacket is now livid dust.

CAKE

On the evening of June 12, 2019, a Wednesday, I find a tick on my nape. I am at my desk absorbed in my work when I feel a slight creeping sensation beneath my collar. My left hand rises automatically to my neck as my right hand continues correcting some long-overdue text. I bring something tiny and black to the lamp-lit paper, then recognize what the weirdly flattened thing is. It is not engorged; it had not yet attached itself. As swiftly and reflexively as I had grabbed it, my pen nib comes to skewer the tick on the white page. Its legs gradually cease squirming. A translucent black fluid oozes from the pinioned insect onto the paper. It is not blood; as I said, it had not yet bitten. It is not quite like ink either. All of this happens smoothly and instinctively; the words *tick, nape, paper, translucence, pen, ink* offer themselves just after the action, as it occurs to me that the dark liquid I am observing is melancholic bile.

This is what I recall of the humours as the tick dies. They are the fluids that circulate through the body, connecting the shifting moods to a cosmologically moistened circuitry. Their collective origin is the liver; their particularities arise with their circulation through various glands and organs. The sanguine person is linked to air in a responsive relationship by a bloodlike fluid originating in the heart, and so is expansive in both body and spirit. Cholerous yellow bile is exuded by the gall bladder, in the bitterness of anger. The phlegmatic humour seems to move with the sleepy coolness of water or lymph. It is stored in the lungs. Only black bile, the fluid of melancholy, whose source is the spleen, has no observable correlative among the various internal fluids of the human body. It is not like chyle or wax or semen or tears; black bile is purely imagined. It is a spurious fluid necessary to supplement and correct the asymmetry of the other three, and thence to connect the cosmical human body to the four worldly elements. The element of melancholy is earth. It is dry and cold. Each of our bodies comprises a unique combination of these four humours in always-shifting proportions; our complexions, dispositions, and health express our humoral balance or imbalance at any time. In my own humoral admixture, what is the exact proportion of melancholy to choler? It may have been a preponderousness of the darkest humour that brought me to this cold house, together with my dog, most melancholic of beasts, as Benjamin reminds in his work on the baroque.

A flea will occasionally cross from my dog's body to mine, and so might have the tick. Or the tick could have fallen directly onto me from the branches of the cherry tree where my dog and I had sheltered from a bout of rain during our morning walk. If it had indeed arrived on me that morning, the tick had spent the long day making its way from my jacket or my loose hair to the bare skin of my nape. We had been eating cherries beneath the tree as it rained, my dog the rotting ones from the ground, me the low-hanging over-ripe ones that were splitting in the wet summer. I did think of Rousseau and his cherry idyll as my dog and I ate – that passage in the *Confessions* where a cherry orchard in full fruit serves as foil for a nascent flirtation. The young Rousseau, on his ladder or his bough, I can't remember which, tosses down cherries for two girls to catch in their out-held skirts. The style then being décolletée, some cherries miss their marks and catch in the girls' soft breasts. If only I were cherries, Rousseau thinks, looking down from his perch at this colourful vision. Or so he wrote. I believe the claim was the retrospective one of the middle-aged writer; it was too neat and humorous for adolescent lust, which could not have changed much between Rousseau's time and ours. And enjoying my idle doubt I continued to eat the burst-open fruits, spitting pips into the wet grass, or sometimes leaving them clinging palely to their stems on the branch, these cherries are so ripe.

I lift my pen. The tick is now a smear. Near my desk, on the little couch I have abandoned to her use, my dog naps, groaning softly from time to time with deep satisfaction. I am familiar of course with Dürer's etching of melancholia, but my image of it is vague, darker even than Dürer's own chiaroscuro, and the only actual detail I can bring to mind from the famous image is the wrinkled or ruffled appearance of the sleeping dog's ears, as if they were the crumpled inner leaves of Batavia lettuces, so unlike my own dog's ears, which remain vigorously upward-pointing like tulip swards, even in sleep. I am curious to look closely again at Dürer's image; I rise to search for the only book in my library I am certain will include it, a fairly recent collection of the translated writings of the mercurial art historian Aby Warburg. I had ordered this book a few years before, especially to read the great scholar's essay on Saturn and melancholy; and so it was because of my arcane interest in the history of melancholia that I came to learn of Warburg's library, his atlas of memory, and the astoundingly compelling mobility of his thought, all of it organized according to the feminized baroque gesture of the serpentine line. This line, moving from antiquity to the present, was called by the Hamburg scholar the 'nympha.'

It is 10:35 p.m. and outside the solstice sky is just darkening. The occasional liquid trill of the season's last nightingales deepens the evening. I hear my neighbours' shutters close.

This is all wrong. It was not 10:35 pm, it was late morning, I was not correcting some unnamed manuscript, I was reading an essay by Benveniste, my dog was not sleeping, she was whining softly near the kitchen door, insisting upon her deferred walk. I was taking notes as I read. The essay was the infinitely gorgeous 'The Notion of Rhythm in Its Linguistic Expression.' Each time I attempt to summarize this essay it reconfigures itself sinuously just beyond my comprehension. I feel for it something like a lover's rapture. Reader, I say this knowing how overblown the sentiment will seem, but when in the first paragraph Benveniste tidily demolishes the conventional etymology of the word *rhythm*, disproving with a precision bordering on arrogance the long-repeated belief that its Indo-European root is related to the natural-seeming alterations of temporality and the regular repeating movement of the waves, at each reading my excitement is physiological and fresh. I know I am about to enter something unimaginably nuanced. He frees rhythm from nature understood as an external, environmental limit and introduces me once again to the human abundance of form. But for Benveniste, following the atomist philosophers, form is not a limit either. Form is a gestural passage that we can witness upon a garment in movement, a face in living expression, or in the mobile marks of a written character as it is traced by the pen. Rhythm, an expression of form, *is* time, but it is time as the improvisation that moves each limited body in play with a world. Not necessarily metrical or regular, it's the passing shapeliness that we inhabit. It both has a history and *is* the history that our thinking has made. As I achieved the apex of excitement in my rereading of this beautiful document, attempting to grasp anew how a concept becomes quite literally a landscape (for only much later in the history of this word had rhythm come to articulate and even make perceivable the repeating or cycling patterns we attribute now to nature), I felt the tick on my neck.

Now I wonder: had the tick begun to write with its bilious ink? What word or phrase was about to be spelled out blindly on the back of my neck? A tick *is* blind; it is also deaf and without even a sense of smell. I had once read that its only sensation is for heat. Dormant on some random foliage, where it exists only to await the hot sense trigger that we animals are, it drops towards the precise temperature of mammalian blood and nothing else. It lives and perceives only for the world our bodily warmth constitutes. Like a melancholic fixing on some abstruse and frail detail to worry it slowly to a psychic wound, once on the host's body, whether dog or human, the tick roams towards the barest, most tender and heated site. I had thought then about the inchoate pleasure of the arrival I had prevented, the punctum, but now I guess at the phantom line I had forestalled, 'only there where I am not,' from *Le Spleen de Paris*, for instance, spelled out by the unculminated nape marks of the spurious black bile.

In Dürer's *Melencolia I*, a winged female with loose hair wreathed in small leafed vegetation sits on a low step, the weight of her leaning head braced by a clenched hand in the clichéd pose of thinking. Her elbow rests on her knee. The folds of her full skirt suggest a slightly stiff fabric, perhaps linen, and where the garment falls over her seat or bench, the fine row of hem-stitching is just visible in faint relief where it slightly puckers the textile. The light is coming from her lower left side, from a source just outside the picture frame, and it reveals, resting against her hip, a chatelaine, the traditional belt worn at a woman's waist, to which she would attach her household keys and purse. Melencolia's heavy skeleton keys are numerous in the image, and below them, at the place where her feet are hidden by the crumpled folds of the gown, is a fabric purse. Its crimped-shut openings are secured by three round buttons wrapped round with dangling ribbons or drawstrings. Melencolia glances up towards the right and her brow is troubled. Many scholars have discussed the meanings of the tools and objects that surround her: the sphere, the hourglass, Saturn's magic square, the scales and ruler and hammer, the long, serrated knife. They especially ruminate over the large, many-faceted geometrical mass to her right, the mysterious polyhedron, behind which a ladder rises diagonally, bisecting the picture plane. The comet-like light in the sky is mentioned, the rainbow, and the gargoylish wisp of cloud that holds aloft the titular word. Melencolia is an unsolved plenum. But I am unaware of any discussion or even notice of the tightly crimped folds of her purse. It's an accessory detail. Yet in this composition each component carries equivalent semantic weight; the ribs of the sleeping dog are no less meaningful than the fine stream of sand in the hourglass, or the flames in the distant brazier, or the rooftops of the far-off village seen through the rungs of the ladder.

Or had the insect succeeded in slightly breaking my nape skin with its barbed, needle-like hypostome? Had it transferred to my bloodstream, mixed with a small quantity of its arachnid saliva, the virus-like paternity of the body of work that I had discovered within myself? It is likewise the contagion of a virus, I have heard, that causes the brindled beauty of the parrot tulip, the peculiar variegation so valuable and sought-after during the Dutch baroque, when tulip bulbs were first brought from Turkey to the Netherlands. In Europe a virus of the common potato – itself only recently introduced, from South America – caused a mutation in the Turkish flowers, expressed in the bizarre striated colouring and feathered form of the petals, now referred to as 'broken.' Now I must wonder whether I did not so much assume the paternity, nor receive it in the mystic transmission whose architecture I have sought so rangingly to comprehend in these pages, so much as I had been infected by it, so that at this very moment the Baudelairean authorship moves in my blood, lymph, chyle, saliva, tears, wax, cyprine, and other fluids.

My interest in humoral theory, begun in an attempt to understand my own splenetic nature, expanded with my move to this isolated hamlet. Here the humours, in their constant mutability, seem like site-specific descriptions of the body's integration of or struggle with earthly time. The windows of my cottage face east and west; I watch the sun rise and set over large fields, and often the farmers are out working in their huge modern tractors with the glassed-in cabs, already as my day begins, or after it ends and I am in bed. I began to see that the landscape, like the sky, is at every point, at every minute, extremely active, never repeating. It is a form of intelligence. Insecticide is being sprayed, wheat is being threshed at midnight, one morning a white powder appears dusted over the plowed-up canola field, in early autumn the wheat will be planted, a premature frost on plowed earth will change the character of the light. The huge, yellow, cylindrical straw bales will be irregularly scattered as far as the horizon, like some giantesque game of chance or a lesson in constructive geometry. And the place of the sunrise will slowly swing from the dark massy smudge that is the oak forest in the mid-distance to, in mid-winter, the rusted roof of the agricultural shelter beside which grows the ancient and bare cherry tree.

When I walk my dog late mornings I discover fruits I have never heard of, on the trees bordering the fields. *Pêche de vigne* that shoots pungent scarlet juices as my teeth puncture the tough brownish skin; leathery medlars, which used to be called openarse, since their calyx end resembles a dark rectum, and which made for marmalade before the importation of citrus fruit to this continent; and the rowan fruit, which becomes sweet only once rotten, and which was used by the poorer people here to make a tannic wine. And the more familiar trees too, the walnuts and sweet chestnuts, and the haws of the eglantine, so that always I come home from our walks with my pockets stuffed, if I have not thought to bring along a little sack for my finds. And these fields and hedges that I walk among are the same ones I see depicted in the paintings I visit in the regional beaux-arts museum. Poussin's fields and riverbanks seem to be precisely the ones I live among, and the same for the unknown and sometimes unnamed minor painters whose works are so interestingly copious in these small museums. In the village churches and funeral chapels, primitive Romanesque frescoes depict scenes from the Book of Revelations, or the woman's temptation at the fruit tree, and the rudimentary yet subtle pigments were made from the local river clays and oxides. These clays too are often used for cures for small ailments – troubled digestion, rashes, rheumatic aches. Landscape is the same as painting, and it is the same as time, and cooking, and medicine, and the economy. I say the same, but that is not precise. What I mean is that all these things mesh to form a fabric, which, like a worn garment, moves, shifts, arranges itself in figures recalling the idiosyncracy and emotion of the face. The notion of a rhythmic cyclicity is an invented concept we deploy from a great distance to placate the intensity and vulnerability of time.

Benveniste, who had been born in Alep, and who spent his life since early childhood studying in Paris, in his last seven years suffered the effects of a stroke, including the loss of his speech, but not his presence of mind. He was forced to abandon his sprawling study of language in Baudelaire. In the years between 1969 and his death he was often visited at the hospital in Créteil by Julia Kristeva, who had been one of his students. Kristeva describes his still-joyous expression on receiving his guests; his face and his laboured ability to gesture with his fine hands were his only means of communication. She recalls specifically a strange incident one afternoon shortly before his death. His sister had contacted her with the message that Benveniste requested her visit. When his old student arrived, he beckoned her to approach him more closely, then with a mischievous smile he began to shakily trace, using his index finger, some letters on her chest. She was flustered and drew away with embarrassment, so he leaned forward and attempted a second time to spell out his undecipherable message on her blouse. Drawing back again, she offered him a pen and paper. With some difficulty he traced out the Greek letters THEO in majuscule. This was Benveniste's last written word. What did god mean to the great linguist and mentor in his speechless final years, written enigmatically, inklessly, in Greek, upon his female student's heart? Was this THEO the meeting between unspoken, interior languages and subjectivity itself, between the subject's experienced 'I' and the 'you' who necessarily received the affective enunciation, between the general capacity towards such an utterance and the experience of the body's limit, as Kristeva later thought? How can we imagine the involuntary seven-year silence and isolation of the linguist of co-subjectivity other than as a profoundly etched chiaroscuro? Was the writing of any word a permanent revolt against structural determination, a plunge into the infinite generosity of signification, the conversion of that generosity to a name?

That afternoon, pausing in my Benvenistean studies, I walked with my dog as usual through the court of a nearby farm. Where the narrow road cut through the middle of the assemblage of stone buildings and sheds, I admired the stacks of disused objects that encrusted the corners and edges of the barn, the orchard, the chicken coop, the woodshed, the tractor hangar: rolls of rusted chicken wire being saved for a mysterious future, the skeletons of old green-painted rabbit hutches collapsed behind tractor tires, bright blue forty-five-gallon oil drums beneath a gnarled peach tree. Behind these barrels I suddenly noticed the farmer, a gentle man with whom I often spoke of the weather, the fruit trees, and the possible meanings of bird migrations. He was hiding a little. He was with his own dog, the sort of large spotted spaniel typically kept for hunting in this region. I saw that the farmer was holding a large wedge of yellow cake in one hand, while with the other he was tenderly and covertly feeding broken-off pieces to his dog. He glanced up and noticed me; we greeted one another. He said that his dog had become heart-sick and would only eat cake.

Baudelaire could pronounce only one word in the final months of aphasic paralysis leading to his death – *crénom*, a mild curse that contracted the holy term *sacré nom*. The poet had suffered a stroke in the baroque church of Saint-Loup in Namur, Belgium, a church he had described as both 'sinister and gallant,' 'the interior of a terrible and delicious catafalque, embroidered in black, rose, and silver.' He fell, on March 5, 1866, in the company of his friends, before a carved wooden confessional, as he praised its impossibly detailed beauty to them. This sacral theatre of revelation and humility is supported by spiralling wooden pillars intertwined with fruiting grapevines all lividly undulating like forms of life. On its screening panels, decorative cartouches are held aloft by hybrid beings of innovative morphology. The result is a pantheistic intoxication, an ensemble of dreams, a disorienting multiplication of strangeness: a new antiquity.

After Saint-Loup, Baudelaire's health declines rapidly. By March 22 he is paralytic. By March 30, he can no longer speak. He's living moneyless in his Brussels hotel in the certitude of expulsion. By the second of July, his friends help him return to Paris by train. They install him in a nursing home, in the company of Manet's portrait of Jeanne Duval. He dies on August 31, 1867, repeating again the curse *crénom*.

'My soul sets out on a long voyage,' said Baudelaire.

'We embody it always as a god, immemorial, elusive and solitary,' said Benveniste of the sea in Baudelaire's poems.

The name, the water, refuse possession. The pronoun refuses possession, and so does the singer. Jeanne Duval, she refuses possession.

The image is not large, but it is proportionately wide – about an arm span, I think. Inside an ornately carved gilt frame a woman half-reclines on a long dark green velvet sofa. Behind her, the top third of the painting is occupied by a transparent white curtain falling in loose folds. The curtain's scalloped lower edge is decorated with floral or botanical embroidery swiftly rendered in curling white brush strokes. Her right hand, fine, strong and alive, rests lightly on the curtain where the filmy fabric is blowing over the back of the sofa, a little lip of strong light caught on the top of her relaxed thumb. She is wearing a black bracelet, perhaps a ribbon tying a cameo or medallion to her wrist, and this simple ornament punctuates her gesture. The rendering is loose and certain. Her left hand, resting on her lap, where it is obscured by the fabric of her white dress, holds a partially closed green-black fan. This dress, buoyant, splendid, creamy, and cool, floats diagonally downwards towards the lower right corner, alive with brushwork. Surely it is a hoop skirt. Almost certainly it is cotton, less transparent than the background curtain, vertically striped with opaque bands, like a damask that throws off violet light. Also, the skirt is an architectural cloud. In the world of this skirt, chalky warm white is irregularly striated and hatched with cool blue-grey, lilac, glimmers of ochre, smears of putty and soot. Beneath the pigment, the suggestion of the shadow of an extended leg. This skirt lifts around her slight body like a frothy element that attaches to the earth only at her high waist. The element of the skirt drifts buoyantly to the southeast. In the close foreground towards the west, her ankles, white-hosed and casually crossed, one foot shod in a low black slipper with a black bow, the other hidden by the hem of her voluminous dress. The perspective places her small face in the shadowed distance. Her brows and eyes are dark suggestions, quickly drawn and deeply expressive. Her black hair is arranged to fall behind her ears, revealing pendant carnelians or rubies. Her mouth is firmly set and her jaw strong. She withdraws from the gaze; she doesn't offer herself to an interpretation. Her autonomy is the very core of beauty. The concentrated intensity of her distant and withdrawn face is a rhetorical counterpoint to the skirt's expansive, forward-tumbling froth. I recognize the future girl in her refusal, her gravitas. She is irreducible to the visible, and she is irreducible to the invisible. She is relaxed in her displeasure. She is totally modern. I'll never know her and she doesn't care. This is Jeanne Duval. She's a philosopher. She was painted by Manet in 1862, a year after Baudelaire had dedicated to her a copy of the second edition of *Les Fleurs du mal*: 'Homage à ma très chère Féline.' Now I meet her image in Paris, on June 13, 2019. The linden trees are in flower. I'm fifty-seven years old. I'm thinking about the immense, silent legend of any girl's life. She's leaning back, observing.

IMAGES

(in order of appearance)

Claude Lorrain, *Odysseus Returns Chryseis to Her Father*, 1644

Claude Lorrain, *Seaport, Effect of Mist*, 1646

Steve Lacy, *Monk's Dream*, 2000

Jean-Luc Godard, *Bande à part*, 1964

Gustave Courbet, *Portrait of Charles Baudelaire*, 1848

Émile Deroy, *Portrait of Charles Baudelaire*, 1844

Gustave Courbet, *The Painter's Studio: A Real Allegory
Summing Up Seven Years of My Artistic and Moral Life*,
1848–1855

Jean-Antoine Watteau, *Pilgrimage to Cythera*, 1717

Vincente Minnelli, *An American in Paris*, 1951

Eugène Delacroix, *Jacob Wrestling with the Angel, Saint Michael
Slaying the Demon, Heliodorus Driven from the Temple*
(Eglise Saint-Sulpice), 1854–1861

Émile Deroy, *La petite mendiante rousse*, 1843

Edward Steichen, *Colette*, 1935

August Sander, *Secretary at West German Radio in Cologne*, 1931

Philippe Halsman, *Georgia O'Keeffe*, 1967

Agnès Varda, *Vagabond*, 1985

Eugène Delacroix, *The Unmade Bed*, 1828

Knock-off Thierry Mugler teal-green viscose skirt suit, 1985

Deborah Turbeville, *Bath House* series, 1975

Christo and Jeanne-Claude, *The Pont Neuf Wrapped*, 1985

John Cassavetes, *Love Streams*, 1984

Baudelairean jacket, black wool and velvet, uncertain
  provenance

T. Eaton Company, slim tailored black jacket, cotton and
  viscose, 1982

Ann Demeulemeester, tailored black wide-lapelled jacket,
  wool crepe, 1994

Comme des Garçons, black bolero jacket, wool and nylon, 2001

Comme des Garçons, black wool gabardine jacket with knitted
  sleeves, 1993

Limi Feu, black gabardine double-breasted jacket with tar
  edging, post-2007 (year uncertain)

Joseph Beuys, *The Pack*, 1969

Albrecht Dürer, *Melencolia I*, 1514

Édouard Manet, *Baudelaire's Mistress, Reclining*, 1862

TEXTS

Sara Ahmed, *Queer Phenomenology: Orientations, Objects, Others*

Alexandre Privat d'Anglemont, *Paris anecdote*

Théodore de Banville, *Mes souvenirs*

Charles Baudelaire, *Correspondance, tome I, II*, ed. Claude Pichois

 Œuvres complètes I, II, ed. Claude Pichois

 The Poems in Prose (tr. Francis Scarfe)

 His Prose and Poetry, ed. T. R. Smith (tr. Arthur Symons, Joseph T. Shipley, F. P. Sturm, W. J. Robinson, Richard Herne Shepherd)

Walter Benjamin, *The Arcades Project* (tr. Howard Eiland, Kevin McLaughlin)

 The Origin of German Tragic Drama (tr. John Osborne)

Émile Benveniste, 'The Notion of "Rhythm" in its Linguistic Expression' (tr. Mary Elizabeth Meek)

 Baudelaire

John Berger, 'Caravaggio, or the One Shelter'

Michèle Bernstein, 'In Praise of Pinot-Gallizio' (tr. John Shepley)

Christine Buci-Glucksmann, *Baroque Reason: The Aesthetics of Modernity* (tr. Patrick Camiller)

Judith Butler, *Bodies That Matter: On the Discursive Limits of 'Sex'*

Champfleury, *Le réalisme*

Gustave Courbet, 'The Realist Manifesto' (tr. Linda Nochlin)

Guy Debord, 'Introduction to a Critique of Urban Geography' (tr. Ken Knabb)

Gilles Deleuze, *The Fold* (tr. Tom Conley)
    Difference and Repetition (tr. Paul Patton)

Therese Dolan, 'Manet's *The Street Singer* and the poets'

Edmond de Goncourt and Jules de Goncourt, *Pages from the Goncourt Journal* (tr. Robert Baldick)

Donna Haraway, 'A Cyborg Manifesto'

Siegfried Kracauer, 'The Hotel Lobby' (tr. Thomas Y. Levin)

Julia Kristeva, 'Émile Benveniste: un linguiste qui ne dit ni ne cache, mais signifie'

Stéphane Mallarmé, 'Le tombeau de Charles Baudelaire'

Karl Marx, *Capital* (tr. Ben Fowkes)

Mira Mattar (Twitter conversation)

Nadar, *Charles Baudelaire intime: le poète vierge*

Charles Olson, *Selected Writings*

Walter Pater, *The Renaissance: Studies in Art and Poetry*

Georges Perec, *Life: A User's Manual* (tr. David Bellos)

Edgar Allan Poe, 'Philosophy of Furnishing'

Marcel Proust, *Sur la lecture*

Thomas De Quincey, *Confessions of an English Opium-Eater*

Jean-Jacques Rousseau, *Emile or On Education* (tr. Allan Bloom)
    Reveries of the Solitary Walker (tr. Peter France)

Severo Sarduy, *Barroco*

Enid Starkie, *Baudelaire*

Stendhal, *Memoirs of an Egotist* (tr. David Ellis)

William Carlos Williams, 'Asphodel, That Greeny Flower'

(Citations from all French-language texts not otherwise attributed have been translated by Lisa Robertson.)

ACKNOWLEDGEMENTS

My gratitude to Jean-Philippe Antoine, Julie Joosten, Kathy Slade, and sabrina soyer, who generously read drafts, responded, and encouraged me in this writing, and also to my editor for the press, Jason McBride. Alana Wilcox has been more than my editor; she trusted a bare sketch of an idea two years ago, and helped it become this book, with her judicious balance of wit, care, and firmness. It is a pleasure for me to be indebted to her. Thanks also to the Foundation for Contemporary Arts, in New York, who by giving me the C. D. Wright Award for Poetry in 2018 supported a full-time year of writing, as well as the furnace that warmed the activity.

Some chapters were first cast as responses to invitations: Carl Lavery and Clare Finburgh asked me to participate in the 2016 colloquium How to Drift, at the Centre for Contemporary Arts in Glasgow; I presented 'Port' as my contribution. 'Windows' was my lecture for the 2016 art-writing conference Never the Same, at the Contemporary Calgary, at the invitation of Lisa Baldissera and Joanne Bristol; Frances Loeffler at the Oakville Gallery commissioned the chapter 'Anywhere Out of the World' for a monograph accompanying an exhibition of the work of the painter Allison Katz, published by JRP Editions. 'Drunk' was commissioned by Jazmine Linklater, Nell Osborne, and Hilary White of the Manchester poetry collective No Matter, for their spring 2019 reading series. The story of the melancholic tick was a response to an invitation by Tiziana La Melia for the commissioned series *Out of Focus*.

Our beloved dog Rosa (2004–2019) was my daily companion in this writing. She died under the linden tree in late August in Nalliers, as I completed my final draft. She's in this book.

ABOUT THE AUTHOR

Lisa Robertson is a Canadian poet and art writer who lives in rural France. Born in Toronto, she began writing, publishing, and collaborating with a vibrant community of poets and artists in Vancouver in the early nineties, and she has continued those activities for thirty years. In 2018, the Foundation for the Contemporary Arts in New York awarded her the inaugural C. D. Wright Award for Poetry.

BOOKS BY LISA ROBERTSON

POETRY

3 Summers
Cinema of the Present
R's Boat
Lisa Robertson's Magenta Soul Whip
The Men: A Lyric Book
The Weather
Debbie: An Epic
XEclogue

PROSE

Nilling: Prose
Occasional Works and Seven Walks from the Office for Soft Architecture
Revolution: A Reader (with Matthew Stadler)

Typeset in Arno and Larish Neue.

Printed at the Coach House on bpNichol Lane in Toronto, Ontario, on Zephyr Antique Laid paper, which was manufactured, acid-free, in Saint-Jérôme, Quebec, from second-growth forests. This book was printed with vegetable-based ink on a 1973 Heidelberg KORD offset litho press. Its pages were folded on a Baumfolder, gathered by hand, bound on a Sulby Auto-Minabinda, and trimmed on a Polar single-knife cutter.

Seen through the press by Alana Wilcox
Edited for the press by Jason McBride
Cover design by Information Office
Cover art and photograph by Lisa Robertson
Designed by Crystal Sikma

Coach House Books
80 bpNichol Lane
Toronto ON M5S 3J4
Canada

416 979 2217
800 367 6360

mail@chbooks.com
www.chbooks.com